To End the Night

Julius Caesar's Secret War

By Lluew Grey

Published by Inicio Press
https://www.iniciopress.com/
To End the Night: Julius Caesar's Secret War

ISBN: 978-1-998315-05-5
         978-1-998315-06-2

Dedication

Always and Forever to my wife!

To quote Madmartigan: "You are my sun, my moon, my starlit sky, without you I dwell in darkness, I love you."

Also to:

My Brothers Jason, Josh, and Warren: Your excitement keeps me going!

My Mother: Your encouragement gives me strength!

My friends Ryan and Barbara: Your love and support mean everything!

And to my friend Hank, the other half of my imagination!

Contents

Chapter 1
January to March 49 BC

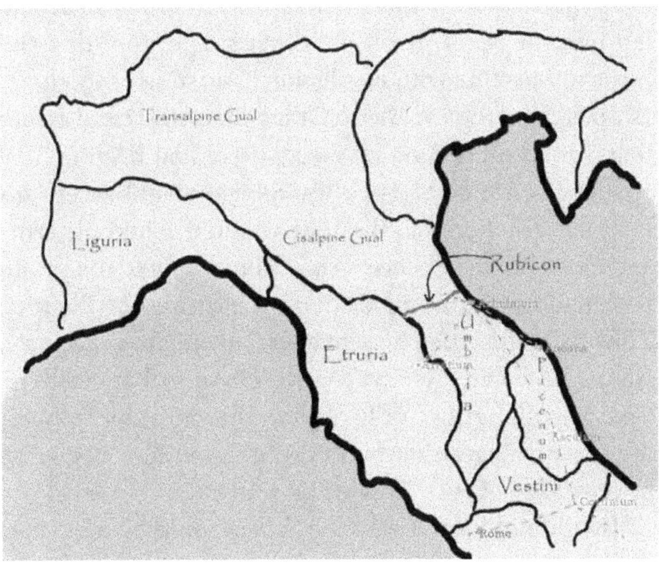

Julius Caesar was growing impatient.

A knock at the door, and Curio entered. Disregarding the weary look of his friend and all attempts at hospitality, Julius demanded an answer from the Senate. Sighing with dread at what his news would bring, Curio answered, "The Senate has ordered that you give up Transalpine Gaul to Lucius Domitius Ahenobarbus and Cisalpine Gaul to Marcus Servilius Nonianus and dismiss your army. They have decreed that you will be branded a traitor if you do not do this immediately."

Stunned silence filled the room. Eventually, Julius replied in bitter tones: "Leave me." Unsure what his friend would do, Curio left, worried and with a heavy heart.

Julius's emotions were conflicted. He did not want to start this war, but his survival instinct was strong, and the Senate's decree left him little choice. The march from Britannia had been long but relatively uneventful; he had left most of his army on the other side of the Alps and come to Ravenna with one legion consisting of 300 horses and 5,000 foot soldiers. Other than the usual issues that armies on the march faced, there had been no real challenges. He had hoped the Senate would accept his first offer. He had told them he would disband his army and enter Rome in peace if they would uphold the promises made to him and disband the armies of Pompey. They had refused, so he sent a second offer to the Senate, stating he would give up the governorship of Transalpine Gaul and all but two of his legions in return for upholding the privileges that had been granted him two years prior, and again, the Senate had refused.

He did not want a war ... but *they* could be most persuasive.

He longed for his youth before he learned of their existence and the plans in store for him. At their direction, he had formed his triumvirate, taken governorship of Gaul, and expanded Roman territory there. He had been absent from Rome for nine years, and everything had changed. He had lost his beloved daughter, his triumvirate had collapsed, his power had been threatened, and *they* wanted it back.

Suddenly, someone was there; Julius was startled with a twitch.

"The news is not good," Julius said.

"It was expected," came the reply in an eerie half-whisper. "The faction backing Pompey is strong, but we will break them and restore the glory of the Vampyre nation."

"Must Rome suffer this war? Is there no other way?" asked Julius, although he believed he knew what the answer would be.

"It must be done for the good of your people and mine. Tomorrow, you will cross the Rubicon with your army. The game must be played." The Vampyre was gone as quickly and silently as he had come.

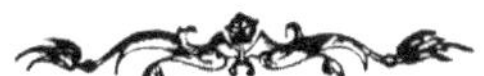

A civil war would cause the death of countless Romans. Was this small faction of Vampyres any better than the rest? They spoke of restoring the balance and returning to the old ways when they had founded Rome, the days of kings, gods, and superstition. Was that any better than the infighting and corruption in the Senate? Everyone knew that something pulled the strings from the shadows; this unspoken knowledge and the unspoken fear that accompanied it had held the people in thrall for centuries, but education, reason, and public discourse had weakened the blind faith that had once kept the people so willingly in hand. Would the masses ever accept that level of superstition again?

He had to get out of the apartments and think. Upon leaving, he went to watch the gladiators but did not see the spectacle, for his mind was elsewhere. He wandered on. Seeking to distract himself, he went to a fencing school. He intended to model his school after schools like this, if only they would let him be. While there, he secretly sent messages for his friends to meet him at the Rubicon after dark. Maybe they would have answers for him, but he could not let his watchers know anything was amiss, so he went to the baths to calm his nerves and give the appearance of normalcy. He went through the motions as if in a fog.

After some exercise, a dip in the tepidarium, and time in the caldarium, he barely noticed when the masseur left; he was led back to the tepidarium and, finally, to the frigidarium. It was only as he dressed that he began to come back to himself. He left the bath and returned to his apartments. Packing some necessities but not enough to arouse suspicion, he went out again. He wandered around Ravenna until it began to grow dark. He took the Rimini gate, as this would be the way out of town they would be least likely to watch. Seeking to ensure he was not followed, he wandered in the dark, not daring to light a torch.

At last, just before daybreak, he arrived at the meeting place on the banks of the Rubicon. This tiny river was the official border between Cisalpine Gaul and the provinces under direct control of Rome. Crossing it with an army was an act of war.

The first friend he saw was Asinius Pollio, followed quickly by the others stepping out of the shadows. He began to cheer up. Surely, he had been surreptitious enough, and the Vampyres were not here; his friends' counsel would be welcome, and together, they would find a way to avoid this war.

He stood for a moment among his friends as they

waited for him to begin. At last, he spoke: "We have a decision to make. We may still retreat, but if we pass this bridge, nothing is left but to fight it out in arms." Instead of answering him, his friends stepped aside. Behind them stood a cloaked and hooded figure. His heart sank. In silence, this graceful stranger led them back to where Caesar's legion was camped and awaiting his orders. The Vampyre strode to a trumpeter, grasped the frightened man's instrument, and sounded the advance.

Caesar pondered the "river" before him, little more than a stream; such a tiny thing to hold so much significance. To bring his army across this border into Italy proper was an irreversible act of rebellion, sedition, and civil war. Caesar shouted with an exuberance he did not feel: "Let us go where the omens of the gods and the sins of our enemies have called us! The die is cast!"

Unbeknownst to him, the Vampyres had sent a messenger to the army hours earlier, commanding in his name that the army be ready to march; thus, the crossing began immediately. They marched in double time and quickly arrived in Ariminum. Along with the surprise and speed of his march, the city government had been infiltrated by Vampyres, who wanted to see his success. After a brief, token resistance, his army surrounded the city, and it was surrendered to his control. His army believed this to be a sign that his revolution would be swift and victorious.

Once Ariminum was taken, he was approached by some tribunes who had taken his side in the debates of the Senate when he had sent his requests. "When we attempted to veto the Senate decree, we were threatened by Pompeian soldiers and forced to flee for our very lives," they told him. "We disguised ourselves as slaves and escaped Rome in a hired carriage." Already, it had begun. His supporters in Rome were displaced and branded as enemies of the state. If crossing the Rubicon hadn't been enough, this also left him no choice but to follow the struggle through to its bitter end. Maybe then he could restore some of what had already been sacrificed on his behalf.

Julius sent a messenger to have his centurions assemble the legion. He stood before them in his finest regalia. "Men!" he shouted. "Today, we have won a great victory. The gods smile upon us, and I am proud of your bravery and the glory you bring to your names. We are not done, though. I have just been brought word from these Senators." He stepped to the side, motioning the tribunes forward. "Many in the Senate were just and true, but a small group of tyrants have unjustly subdued their fellow Senators using threats and violence." He paused to let his words sink in. "Through this illegal and unjust coercion, they have passed a decree. They seek to remove my dignitas, my generalship, and the finest soldiers in all of Rome, branding us traitors. I will not accept this. I will not submit until your names and families receive the recognition, glory, and honor you have earned these past nine years. We must not rest until Rome is restored, free from the oppression of this vile minority and their puppet, Pompey! For the glory of Rome, the Second and Fifth cohorts shall take Ancona, the Third and Fourth shall take Arretium. The First shall remain here with me while the rest spread the news in the surrounding countryside: Umbria has been freed by my decree!" The cheering of the soldiers was deafening as they cried out for the glory of Rome and the glory of Caesar.

Walking toward his tent, he began to strip his armor

and hand the pieces to his attendants. He glanced to the side and saw that Curio was still with him. "Dispatch riders to bring word to our armies in Gaul. They are to meet us here expeditiously." With that, he retired to his tent, exhausted. He remained unconvinced that this was the best path for Rome. But what could he do? He had already committed treason by bringing his army this far, and the threats from his shadowy Vampyre overlords were ever-present. Never to be openly acknowledged, these dark puppeteers claimed dominion over Rome and its people; everything and everyone was theirs to do with as they pleased.

For now, the best he could do was to secure his base of operations and await his reinforcements from Gaul. With only the Thirteenth cohort at his disposal, the relatively small and rural region of Umbria was all he could hope to hold; there were only three very small cities, and he already held the largest, Ariminum. Ancona and Arretium had no standing armies, so the cohorts he had dispatched were sure to be victorious.

The weeks wore on. He raged silently at his predicament, torn between his pride, his love of Rome, and fear of his Vampyre Masters. Word trickled in of local victories, and his cohorts slowly returned until he finally received word that all of Umbria was secure. He sat in his darkened tent and prepared to congratulate the troops. Looking for the right words to inform them that they would be marching on shortly after the armies from Gaul arrived, he stiffened as he suddenly felt he was being watched.

"It is about time you noticed me," came the familiar voice. "As a soldier, you should be more aware of your surroundings."

"Are you here to insult me, or do you have a higher purpose?" grumbled Caesar. The Vampyre clicked its tongue in disapproval and paused until Julius bowed his head in deference.

"You will make a new offer," Caesar was told. "Tell them you will give up your governorship and disband your armies. Tell them you will enter Rome as a private citizen and seek the consulship." Julius was stunned. He had begun their war, and all was going well. Lives had been lost; sacrifices had been made. Now they wanted him to give up? "You will ask only this: demand that Pompey leave Italy, remove himself to Spain, and disband his armies in Italy."

"Why have me do this?" Julius struggled to keep his temper in check. "Why now, when the war has begun?"

"They will refuse," whispered the Vampyre. "Pompey has already evacuated Rome. He plans to let you take Italy and attack you from east and west. The people feel abandoned and betrayed. You will show you are willing to stop this war and become a hero to the people." With that, the Vampyre departed.

Summoning a scribe and messenger, Julius carefully dictated the terms. He was so furious that he refused to commit it to writing in his own hand. Upon dispatching the message, he settled in for a long wait; nothing happened quickly in the Senate. He was doubly surprised when the reply came swiftly and in his favor. They would agree to his demands; he had only to withdraw to Gaul while Pompey departed. Relieved that he would not have to carry on this civil war, he sat back and imagined going back for his consulship, starting his fencing school, and fathering as many boys as possible. Shaking himself from his reverie, he began composing a speech to his men; he would spin it as a victory. The Senate had conceded. Their dignity and honor would be restored.

He spent hours choosing the right words to inspire his men. This speech would be a historic moment and needed to be perfect. He wrote and revised until he was sure the history books would proclaim this as one of the great moments of the Republic. Late in the night, as he was nearing completion, a cool breeze preceded dark visitors in his tent. This was the first time he had seen more than one. He recalled the proud day when he was fifteen and gave up the children's praetexta and donned the man's toga. That was the day he had been approached by his first unearthly visitor, and never had he seen more than one at a time since.

"Good. You're here," he stated with a confidence he did not feel. "You were wrong. They accepted the proposal. I will retreat to Gaul while Pompey withdraws to Spain."

The response was biting and immediate. "You will not! You will refuse the Senate and press your attack."

Confused by this, Julius hesitated, and as he hesitated, he grew angry. They had forced his hand again and again. He had done all that they asked and had won what they wanted. Why would they ask him to refuse his victory? Suddenly, he did not care. He was done doing their bidding. Anger had overcome fear. "No!" he growled. "I am a better statesman than Pompey! Accepting this offer will remove all power from Rome! I will win my case in the courts and be consul. You have what you want. I will have the power in the Senate that you need. It is done!"

Before he could take his next breath, Julius found himself dangling from the hand of one of the visitors. Strange and feral eyes staring from beneath its cowl bore into him. Julius's blood ran cold. How could they move that fast? Where did these emaciated bodies get their strength? He was frozen with fear as his soul was laid open to this piercing stare. Hissing and whispers filled the room.

"Finish him!"

"How dare this mere human defy us!"

And most chilling of all: "His blood is of more use to us than his insolence. Kill him."

But a powerful voice drowned out all the rest, barely a whisper. "Silence, fools! This tool is the product of years of planning. He will follow our commands!" Again, the eyes burned into him. "Do not forget, Caesar. You are not the only one under our command. Your army, friends, and family could sustain our hunger for years. You will do as you are told. Your understanding is not required, merely your obedience." Gulping for air, Julius was more frightened than he had ever been. It was then that he knew he was lost. He would do whatever these things asked of him. He nodded his acquiescence. He was slowly lowered to the floor and allowed to catch his breath. "Do as you're told," came the barely audible command. "It is for the good of both our worlds." And they were gone, leaving Julius alone to collect his thoughts.

The Vampyres had always led him to success in the past. They instructed him on how to defeat the rebel Spartacus. They had removed his body and manipulated events so that Pompey and Crassus would have to form the triumvirate with him and get him elected consul. Their advice and manipulation were as responsible for his rise from a disgraced family to one of the most powerful men in all of the Republic as his prowess in battle and ability to inspire men. While he hated them, he also recognized their boon in his life. He let out a big sigh and opened his eyes.

Scrapping his victory speech, Julius instead prepared to continue the war.

At first, there was no resistance. His armies moved south from Umbria into Picenum. Towns opened their gates and welcomed him. The troops left behind in Pompey's hasty retreat happily joined his forces, swelling his numbers. In no time, the whole of Picenum was his. He continued south toward Rome. In the province of Vestini, the city of Corfinium provided his first real resistance. The famous general Domitius Ahenobarbus was ensconced in the town with eighteen thousand men arranged in thirty cohorts. These were new troops unseasoned in war compared to Caesar's battle-hardened soldiers. The numbers were against him, but Julius knew he would win. He had his troops surround the city and waited. He received no guidance from his Masters and did not want to slaughter these men. As much as he hated their commander, the men were blameless and did not need to die. After seven days of siege, the legionaries received word that Pompey had abandoned Rome and fled south toward Brindisi. The next evening, devastated by the understanding that the Republic had no intention of sending reinforcements, Domitius Ahenobarbus surrendered the city.

Rather than take the chance that his men would loot and pillage, Julius left the city surrounded until morning. He contemplated what to do with his old enemy Domitius and the Senators in the town. He feared that the Vampyres would arrive and demand that he put them to the knife, yet no word came.

The next morning, he had Domitius, the Senators, and the wealthy citizens called Equites brought before him. As he was about to address them, he spotted several cloaked and hooded figures scattered throughout the crowd. His overlords were watching him. Lacking direction from the Vampyres on the disposition of prisoners, Julius took a gamble; he would test the statement "for the good of the people." Rather than execute them, he told the captives to learn from their mistakes and, in the future, repay favors in kind. He returned the confiscated military funds and ordered the defending soldiers to be paid. With a wave, he dismissed them and walked away.

Let us see how my "Masters" respond to that, he thought. *I will do what is right as often as I can. I owe at least this much to Rome.*

He retired to his apartments in dread, fearing repercussions from the Vampyres. He contemplated what he knew. The Vampyres had factions that disagreed about how to run Rome. This had often led to wars, which were always violent and bloody. People didn't realize that the Vampyres were behind Sulla's gory revolution, which had resulted in most of the Senate being declared enemies of the state and slaughtered in the streets. They had backed Pompey in his youth when he had become known as "The Butcher." They had never allowed such clemency and compassion for the people as he had shown today. What would his puppet Masters make of that?

One was already seated in his chair as Julius entered the room. "Well done, servant," it said. "Some of my colleagues were less than pleased with your display of mercy. They called it a weakness, but they understand this will set us apart. Our mercy will show our superiority. Our victory will be sure, as we will have the hearts of the people. Continue with your plans, and Rome will be ours. You will see that your people will do well under our rule. They will not need to fear us so long as the blood flows in the arena or on the altars of the gods. The blood is what we need. So long as we have it, your family will prosper." It stood slowly and walked out the door.

This was new. No display of power, no disappearing, no orders, no threats? It had seemed pleased! Still, it had taken credit for his decisions. It was *his* mercy, not theirs, and it would be *his* victory. What had they done to earn these claims? They had done nothing but hide in the shadows and threaten the people he loved. Despite this new development, Julius hated them. *Hated them.* He hated them with every ounce of his soul, and he would find a way to rid the world of their kind. *They must have a weakness. Why else do they hide in the shadows instead of ruling in the open, and what did they do with all the blood? Do they have strange gods who give them powers in return for the blood of humans?* He drifted to sleep, dreaming of a Rome free of these shadowy puppeteers.

In the morning, he awoke with a fresh outlook. Until he could find their weakness, he would take advantage of this unexpected attitude toward clemency. He drafted a letter to his office in Rome stating that his policy would be merciful and magnanimous. He would show the people he was kind to his friends, swift in his victory over his opponents, and merciful once that victory was obtained.

Armed with the knowledge that Pompey and the opposing Senators had been moving down the coast to make the crossing to Greece, Caesar dispatched some men to Rome to prepare for his entrance and sped down the coast to Brindisi. If only he could cut them off before they fled Italy the war would be won!

He moved as fast as he could; his seasoned soldiers were used to a forced march, but the speeds he drove them to were exhausting. His confidence soared as they tore up the miles between him and his prey. Despite his best plans and record speeds, they arrived in Brindisi too late. As they surrounded the city, the ships carrying the Senators to Greece could be seen sailing away near the horizon. Pompey sent out a refusal to meet with him in the absence of the senate. Lacking a fleet, he surrounded the city by land and began construction on floats to block the harbor. After nine days, the ships returned from Greece. With his blockade only half complete, they were easily able to enter the harbor. Pompey fortified the city gates and sent another refusal to meet. While his men set about preparing for an extended siege, Pompey secretly took his closest advisers and all the ships to Greece. Caesar watched from the shore as his last hope for a swift and decisive victory sailed away. When they realized what Pompey had done, the people of Brindisi signaled a surrender from the top of the guard towers. The last of the opposition in Italy had left. Caesar, lacking ships, was unable to pursue Pompey across the Adriatic and decided he would march on Spain, where the bulk of Pompey's armies were. He intended to take advantage of the fact that General Pompey was separated from his armies. First, he would defeat the armies without a general. Then, he would sail to Greece and defeat the general without any armies!

Before he could finish with Pompey, however, he had to finish securing Italy proper. With no armies or leaders remaining, he didn't have to fight for it, just occupy it for it to be his. So, he would take Rome himself and send a junior command to take Sardinia. Curio was dispatched with three legions to secure Sicily and its grain supply. He instructed Curio to leave a token force in Sicily and move on to the provinces in Africa afterward.

Caesar had sent orders as he marched to Brindisi that the free men in his provinces in Gaul should be given full Roman citizenship, and he was anxious to see the bill enacted. He also wanted to win the support of the famed orator Cicero, who had been none too silent in his condemnation of Julius and this civil war. Caesar had great respect for the man and wanted his support and guidance. The notices stating that he intended for the Senate to meet upon his arrival in Rome had gone out.

Caesar departed Brindisi with a small group of men and headed north toward Rome. He made a brief stop back in Corfinium and took the road heading west to Rome. It was then that Cicero met him along the way. Caesar smiled at the influential statesman, thrilled that he would meet with him. Holding out his arm in greeting, he anticipated friendship and support. Rather than grip Caesar's arm, Cicero stopped short.

"I will not go to Rome with you," Cicero stated. Stunned, Caesar's smile vanished. What game was this? Surely, Cicero knew what was at stake.

"At least come and speak for peace!" Julius begged.

"I will do so if I may speak my mind freely," Cicero replied.

"Of course. Who am I to tell you what to say?"

"I will tell them it would be a mistake to send troops to Spain or an army to Greece. I will speak against your war and condemn the situation you have put Pompey into."

Caesar's heart stopped. This was not the support he had hoped for. Who was pulling Cicero's strings? Had another faction of Vampyres gotten to him, or was the man truly ignorant of what was happening? "This does not help me," Caesar said. "I do not want the Senate to hear this."

At last, Cicero smiled. "And this is why I cannot come to Rome."

This small gesture was not enough. "Think again, Cicero. If you will not support and advise me in this, there are others who will," Caesar threatened. Hurt and angry, he stormed away from the man he had most hoped to win to his cause.

Upon his triumphant arrival in Rome, the tribunes who had fled to him in Ariminum convened the Senate. Attendance was not what he had hoped. Most of the Senators remaining in Italy would not leave their estates. Only three of them had come. Still, he tried to win them over. He pointed out the wrongs that had been done to him. He spoke at length of his attempts at peace. For three days, he tried to sway them, and for three days, he grew frustrated and angry. This was not how he expected to be received. Every day that he waited was a day that Pompey's armies in Spain had to prepare. It was a day that Pompey himself had to win support. He needed to complete his conquest of Rome quickly. He needed to have all of Rome behind him if he was going to be able to find a way to fight the Vampyres. Finally, on the fourth day, he broke off the session in a rage. What did he care what these imbeciles thought? "From now on," he stated, "all decisions will be made by me! Martial law is in effect." Caesar was in no mood to be trifled with. Martial law would give him the authority he needed to finish this foolishness with Pompey. He could win back any popularity it lost him after the war had been won.

In his anger, he gathered a small contingent of soldiers and headed for the temple of Saturn, where he knew there was a large treasure that he needed to fund the war. As he arrived at the temple, the Tribune Metellus stepped into his path.

"Stand aside!" Caesar demanded.

Metellus squared his shoulder and spoke. "As a tribune of the people, I cannot let you take this treasure."

"I will only tell you this one time, Metellus. Stand aside or die. It is far more difficult for me to threaten you than to carry out that threat."

"This treasure belongs to the people, not to you, and it's not meant to fund a war for your pride."

Julius shoved the tribune aside in a moment of rashness that would cost him his much sought-after adoration from the people. He ordered his men to break down the door to the temple, then went inside and removed the people's riches. Having obtained the funds he needed, Julius had only to leave loyal allies in charge so he could be free to conclude this war.

He installed his friend Marcus Aemilius Lepidus as marshal of the city on his behalf. Lepidus was a praetor in the Senate and a member of the College of Pontiffs in the state religion of Rome. Leaving him in charge of the city would help sway the Senate, the Clergy, and the people. He then appointed Marcus Antonius (Marc Antony), his cousin and one of his most trusted generals, in charge of Italy and its remaining legions.

On the eve of his departure, Caesar lay in bed unable to sleep. His mind raced with plans and possibilities. He thought of the war with Pompey, and he dreamed of a new age for his people. He would lead a golden age of reason and prosperity, free from the yoke of oppression. Though he was surrounded by friends and supporters, he felt alone. He alone knew the extent of the Vampyre threat and would do what must be done. The Vampyres may be an open secret in Rome, but few knew the extent of their influence or their supernatural aspects. If the Plebeians knew what he knew, there would be panic and riots, and Rome would fall apart. *For the good of Rome*, he thought, *I will carry this burden myself.* Let them think of him what they would. He, Gaius Julius Caesar, would win this war and find a way to free Rome from the bonds of evil that had enslaved it from the beginning.

After a sleepless night, he arose and ordered his legions to be mobilized and prepared to set off for Pompey's provinces in Spain. He had been campaigning in Gaul for nine years and was well prepared for this. His armies were seasoned and strong. Victory would be his. Pulled in two directions simultaneously, Caesar felt he needed to focus on consolidating his power in Rome first. He had to end this civil war once and for all. Only then could he find a way to end his people's slavery to these mysterious, blood-thirsty puppet Masters.

Chapter 2
April 49 to January 48 BC

Pompey had three legates commanding seven legions in Spain. Fortunately for Caesar, the commands were rewarded for sycophants rather than capable commanders. The scholar Marcus Varro was a famous scholar who had lent his influence to Pompey and had little to no experience in warfare. He had been given command of two legions and the income due to that status. The remaining five legions were under the joint command of Lucius Afranius and Marcus Petreius. Petreius had ample experience as a soldier in many campaigns, but this was his first command; it had been given as a reward for loyalty. Afranius was a politician and former consul who had been a strong voice for Pompey in the Senate and was more famous for his dancing than any qualities needed in a general or leader. Although the troops in Spain were experienced soldiers, Caesar had every confidence in his victory.

As he marched from Rome, continuing his campaign, Caesar sent word for his legate in Transalpine Gaul, Quintus Fabius Maximus, known as Fabius, to take charge of the three legions remaining there and take the passes

through the Pyrenees. Caesar and his armies departed overland. The march back through Italy was quick.
Rather than planning his attack on Pompey's troops as
he knew he should have been, his mind was elsewhere.

He had come to recognize one particular Vampyre
among those who occasionally visited him. This was the
one who always spoke of the good of both peoples. He
was the only one who seemed to suggest a synergistic re-
lationship. He had seen this Vampyre more often since
leaving Rome. Who was this Vampyre? He was different.
He listened. He did not appear as ruthless. In fact, the
Vampyre faction's goals seemed to be tempered recently.

*Think, Gaius, where did you first see this one? He had ap-
peared on the march through Gaul from Britannia.*

Britannia.

Why had the Vampyres insisted on this truce with the
Britons? He could have defeated them. His mind raced
around these questions. His preoccupation continued
until he reached Massilia. He expected the Greek colo-
ny would welcome him with open arms, and he would
rest his troops before continuing the march. To his great
surprise, the city gates were closed, and the officials came
to inform him that though he had been a great patron of
the city, so had Pompey. They intended to remain neu-
tral rather than take sides in a Roman conflict. Forced out
of his thoughts of Vampyres to confront the realities of
the war in progress, he was angered by this development.
Nevertheless, Caesar made his camp outside the city, determined to allow his troops to rest.

Showing their words to be traitorous lies, the city allowed his old enemy, Domitius, to enter the harbor and
organize defenses supporting Pompey. Barely able to
contain his fury yet unwilling to waste time in his pursuit

of Spain, Caesar organized a siege of the city. He placed Trebonius in charge of the siege on shore, instructing him to cut off the city and build engines to bring down the walls. He gave command of another contingent to his longtime friend, Decimus Junius Brutus Albinus, known as Brutus. Brutus was to build a fleet on the shores of Massilia and cut off the city from the sea. Content with the plans he put in place and confident in the leaders he left behind, Julius left with the bulk of his forces to continue his march on Hispania.

The rest of the approach to Spain was a simple march; Fabius had already cleared the passes through the Pyrenees. Soon, he would face trained Roman soldiers. Unlike his victories in Gaul and his easy conquest of Italy, he would now have to contend with trained, battle-hardened soldiers. Their lack of competent generals was all that gave him the edge.

In June, Fabius arrived at Ilerda on the River Sicoris and set up camp on the east bank while the enemy amassed on the west. For weeks, they faced each other on opposite banks. With supplies running low, troops were dispatched on regular foraging expeditions. Fabius had even dispatched men to the Northeast to erect two bridges to the other bank. This ensured fighting would not be limited to the bridge at Ilerda.

When Caesar arrived in mid-June, the battle had been limited to a few minor skirmishes. Upon surveying the land, he left a small contingent to the Northeast to protect the camp and bridges. The bulk of his army marched to the bank opposite the enemy camp. Seeing this challenge, Afranius and Petreius employed their men halfway down the ridge to the river. Both armies stood staring at each other across the water, neither willing to start the battle.

Soon, heavy rains began to overflow the already swollen banks. Caesar's bridges collapsed, and the Pompeian forces broke for the River Ebo, hoping to escape the fight for a more tenable position.

Caesar soon had cavalry across the banks in pursuit. The heavily ladened forces of Afranius could not outpace his light cavalry and were forced back toward their camp. Realizing that crossing the Ebo would be impossible, the enemy retreated to the south, attempting to make it through a mountain pass before Caesar could readjust. Again, the troops and the baggage train were no match for the lightning speed of Caesar's army. Afranius and Petreius soon found themselves trapped inside the mountain pass, blocked from any retreat. Caesar dug in, unwilling to slaughter his countrymen if it could be avoided.

After weeks of standoff, Caesar's men were getting impatient, wondering why they did not fight. The Vampyres had been insistent that he was to finish this fight and move on, but he was unwilling to slaughter his countrymen. Fortunately, he did not have to wait much longer before he had his chance. His opponents were surrounded and in a poor position. After four more days, one of the opposing commanders, Afranius, requested a meeting, which Caesar immediately granted.

They met in the open with both armies gathered. Julius stood silently, his jaw tight and his eyes boring into Afranius.

"We are beaten," the commander admitted. "Our duty to Pompey is done. We have no food, and our water is nearly gone. We ask only that you show us the mercy you showed in Corfinium."

"You say you have done your duty?" Caesar laughed.

"You may have discharged your obligation to defend, but you have failed in a greater duty, which I attend with the utmost diligence. Even your famed Pompey has done this duty by fleeing a hopeless situation in Italy." His tone was hard, and his features were still as he continued. "I speak of your obligation to the people, your soldiers, and Rome. I speak of your most sacred duty, the duty to spare the citizens and to see that every possible chance for peace is taken." Lucius looked to the ground, face flushed, unable to meet Caesar's gaze. Seeing his effect, Julius continued. "Pompey is an ungrateful fool filled with jealousy. He seeks the glory I have earned by right. I, among Rome's great generals, have been denied my right to return in triumph. I should have been hailed a hero for what I have done for the Republic. Instead, Pompey and his Senate cronies have attempted to illegally strip me of what is mine and bar me from my right to seek the consulship. By doing this, they have wronged me and the people." Caesar now spoke loudly enough to ensure his words would spread among the armies and the people. "As for your mercy, you shall have it. Even now, my soldiers are returning any plunder taken. Monies shall be repaid, and you shall be free. I will not press your men into service; they are free to leave. Those wishing to raise their standards for the good of the people may add their strength to mine. Those too selfish and shortsighted to do what must be done may go. Either way, your armies are disbanded and must leave this province immediately. If ever we meet across the battlefield again, remember what I have told you. If you repeat this mistake, you will have no mercy from me!"

Having crushed the bulk of Pompey's forces in Spain, word soon flooded in of Spanish towns pledging their allegiance to Caesar. The remaining forces with Varro disbanded, and Spain was his.

Julius sent word that councils would be held in Corduba and Tarraco. He would reward those who supported him and correct those who did not. True to his word, Julius showed leniency to those who had earned it in Corduba and Tarraco. He then put a new governor in place and marched for Rome, anxious to put this civil war behind him and fight the true enemy of the people: the Vampyres. He was also nervous that the Vampyres would continue to demand more sacrifices than he was willing to make.

Any feeling of accomplishment or victory was soon quashed. The Vampyres just would not leave him alone. This spine-chilling visitor was not the spokesman he had become accustomed to but a different, fiercer creature than he had ever seen before.

"You linger too long in Spain," it growled. "You show too much mercy and prolonged the fighting to do so. Slaughter them when the opportunity is there. Word of your ruthlessness will spread, and others will surrender rather than risk your wrath. When they surrender, slaughter their leaders as an example. Save your mercy for the common cattle; they will still love you for it."

Julius reddened. He knew why they wanted the carnage, and he would not give it to them. "You have had plenty of blood during this campaign. I must keep the people on our side so I can hold Rome. Let me do the job you have given me. Rome will be mine if you do not interfere."

"You grow too bold, puppet," the Vampyre replied.

"Rome is ours; you hold it for us at our pleasure." Suddenly, the Vampyre was on top of him, its foul breath heavy on his face, its disturbing eyes boring into his soul, as its cool forehead pressed against his sweaty brow. "Do not forget we have made you what you are and give you all you have. What is given can be taken away. Do not mistake the latitude we have given you thus far for weakness. You will do as you are told or weep as we take your world apart around you. Finish this and move on. We grow weary of your sniveling." Then, it was gone. Nothing remained but flickering candles and the lingering stench of death.

Hot-faced and trembling, Julius renewed his resolve. Almost feeling pity for Pompey, his anger swelled. He knew he must finish this revolution and take the battle to the evil that terrorized all of Rome.

On the return march, he stopped in Massilia, where the city continued to hold out against the siege. As his victorious forces approached, the city surrendered. He confiscated their ships, weapons, and communal treasure for their betrayal but left them their independence and once again denied his soldiers their right to loot. This caused much contention among the men, and a few began to grumble about the long marches, lack of combat, and no rewards. The grumbles got worse as he immediately put them back on the march, declared his intention to stop briefly in Rome, and quickly pushed to Brindisi and continued the campaign in Greece. Caesar was determined to finish this war and was sure his men could see the greater good; they would rest when it was done.

Along the march back to Italy, he attempted to encourage his men with rousing speeches about glory, making history, and saving the Roman Republic. In his mind, the men were proud and happy to sacrifice for the good of the Republic. They were loyal to their commander and would not flinch to do their duty.

His faith was misplaced. His men revolted.

In Northern Italy, the Ninth Legion refused to break camp and march. A delegation was sent to him from the soldiers. "We will not move on until we receive the rewards you have denied us," they declared. "We have marched longer and faster than you have asked of any army before. You have shown more mercy and kindness to the enemy than us. You have denied us our right to plunder and take the rewards of war, and you have intentionally prolonged this war by refusing to allow us to press the attack when victory would have easily been ours. This war has become for the good of Caesar. You claim to be fighting for us but are the only one who benefits."

Caesar glared at the soldiers. How many times could he be surprised by the selfishness and shortsightedness of men? Did they not see that taking plunder and killing unnecessarily would have created more enemies to fight instead of more soldiers in their ranks? This insistence on antiquated custom was ridiculous. "By custom, it is my right as your commander to decimate any legion in rebellion and dismiss the remaining troops with no compensation. Today, one-tenth of your number shall die, and tomorrow, the remaining shall go home in shame."

It was the soldiers' turn to be surprised. Their beloved general had always treated them with regard. Could he not see the abuses he was piling on them? Why deny them their plunder? Worse, why decimate and send them away? They did not want to lose face, nor did they want to leave his service or die. "Please," they begged, "we are tired. We do not want to leave your service. This refusal was ill-advised. We rescind our demands. We will march with you."

Julius sneered. "It is too late for that now. If I show you mercy, others will be encouraged to mutiny. You will be an example. You claim you do not want to lose honor, yet your selfishness today has already cost you."

The soldiers continued to beg forgiveness until Caesar, at last, agreed to a compromise. He demanded the names of those who had fomented the rebellion. He would decimate the instigators alone. After the names were given, Julius held a brief trial. One of the accused men proved that he had not been present. The officer who put his name forth took his place among the condemned. True to his word, one-tenth of the mutinous leaders were executed, and the remaining were sent home as unfit for service. Saddened by the necessity of this act, he once more spoke to the men, imploring them to see the necessity of what they were doing and warning them that rebellion was the same as joining with the enemies of Rome.

The march for Rome continued with Julius more determined than ever to resolve the conflict and restore Rome to its glory. Because Pompey and his Senators had fled and no authority remained, Julius had been appointed dictator in his absence. One of his first orders of business during his eleven-day stay in the city was to hold elections for consul. He was elected with the Senator Publius Servilius Isauricus as co-consul. Isauricus had been one of the Senators who had argued for him from the beginning. His was the legal right, and Pompey and his cohorts were the outlaws.

While he maintained his dictatorship, Caesar was eager to pass some laws. The first was to forgive those whom Pompey had exiled. This would provide him with more loyal and influential allies in Rome. He needed strong allies if he was going to finish this war with Pompey and end the Vampyre menace once and for all. Not oblivious to the war's ravages on the common man, he also passed laws to relieve them. He had all debtors' property and belongings assessed at the highest prewar value, allowing debts to be paid at the newly restored values while lowering all interest rates. Additionally, he passed a law abolishing the hoarding of wealth, decreeing that no man should have more than 15,000 denarii. After confiscating more treasure from the temples and distributing food to the common people, Caesar renounced his dictatorship in favor of the consulship he had won in legally held elections.

During his stay in Rome, Caesar was surrounded by the Senate and the people. Marc Antony was almost always by his side, as was Marcus Brutus, the son of his mistress, Servilia. This constant whirlwind of commotion and companionship prevented his "Masters" from intruding. He was proud that he could do what he thought was right and basked in the open adoration given to him by the common folk of Rome.

Chapter 3
January to September 48 BC

It was the night before he was to depart for Brindisi. Although his stay had been short, his affairs in Rome had been resolved. He put his puppet co-consul Isauricus in charge of the Republic while he finally traveled to Greece to finish Pompey. With this last bit of civil matter taken care of, he could focus on the true menace. As he prepared to retire for the night, the Vampyres returned. Three of them stood in his room; two silent ones flanked the speaker whose voice he had come to know.

"You are doing well, but it was foolish of you to relinquish the dictatorship and cater to the masses," he was told. "Your fortune does not carry everywhere. Curio is dead and has lost Africa. Illyria has been taken, and Pompey's fleet holds the Adriatic. Your pathetic attempts to save your enemy must end. Our goals are within reach. Finish this." And then they were gone again. Only one lingering whisper remained, obviously spoken by one of the others as they left, and it chilled him to the bone: "Thank you for your offering. The soldiers you executed were exquisite."

Caesar was overtaken with shame. He was so focused

on the immediate goals he had nearly forgotten how truly evil these beings were. It had been within his rights to decimate the Ninth for its rebellion, and he had been proud of his forbearance in only decimating the instigators, but now he regretted his actions. He would have to be careful to find a way to do what must be done without leaving blood behind for these vile creatures. Could it be true of Curio? He hadn't heard from the man, but that was to be expected; he wouldn't have been able to send much word while campaigning in Africa, but the forces he had sent him with should have been more than sufficient. Curio was an experienced general. This should not have happened. He could not, however, afford to delay. The Vampyres were right; he must finish this. The civil war must be finished so that nothing could keep him from liberating Rome from the Vampyre yoke that held it in thrall.

The march to Brindisi was a blur. He had allowed himself to be influenced yet again. He had dropped his guard and fed the evil that controlled him. He could not think of what alternatives there had been. He could not let his troops turn into an undisciplined rabble—he must have control over his army—or all was lost. Furthermore, he started to wonder who else they had gotten to. Had they fomented the rebellion? Were all his men his, or would some generals break from him if he displeased his Masters?

Upon arriving in Brindisi, he took stock of the army he had gathered: twelve legions and over one thousand horses, a good army to advance his cause in Greece. A problem arose when he realized he did not have the ships to transport them all in one trip. To bring as many as possible, Caesar took a gamble. He told his men they should leave their slaves and excess baggage in Italy. He promised a swift victory and ample generosity when they had won. Upon hearing this, the legions sent up such a roar of approval that he was sure they had gotten the attention of the gods.

Even with trimming the fat from his train, he still managed only seven legions in the initial crossing. He left Antony and a few other trusted men in charge of the remainder of the army with orders to continue building ships and join him as soon as possible. He knew this was a desperate gamble, but it was certain his better-trained and battle-hardened forces would be more than a match for whatever Pompey had managed to muster in Greece.

Upon landing, he seized several small towns but could not reach Dyrrachium—a city Caesar knew to be a stronghold for Pompey—before the opposing forces cut him off. So, he dug in to wait for Marc Antony and his forces that had been left behind in Italy. While waiting, he sent emissaries to Pompey to attempt peace again. He told Pompey that he could not hope to win and the law was on Caesar's side. He bid Pompey to dismiss his armies and join him for the good of Rome, but Pompey would not hear of it.

"What good would my freedom be," he said, "if the whole world knew it was at your mercy? I would have no power of my own, and the Senate would be a joke subject to the whim of Caesar."

Julius had to wonder if Pompey's jealousy and greed stopped him from accepting peace or if he, too, was controlled by others.

This stalemate between Caesar and Pompey could not last. The longer he waited, the more troops Pompey could gather from the east. Yet without the fullness of his army, he could not hope to defeat Pompey in open battle. As the allotted time for his reinforcements' crossing came and went, Caesar began to worry. Had Pompey's fleet destroyed his army? Had the Vampyres gotten to his generals and swayed them to a different cause? Did the Vampyres know he was searching for information about them? Were they abandoning him because they knew of his betrayal? His impatience and fears got the better of him. In the dark hours of the morning, he commandeered a small craft and set off for Brindisi.

The wind picked up as they began to cross, and the waves became choppy. Soon, the storm had grown so fierce that the captain begged to turn around and head for the safety of the harbor. But before he could respond, a Vampyre appeared on deck and cried, "Do not fear the storm! You are ferrying Caesar; our fortune is greater than this storm!" The captain returned to his duties, trying to keep the craft afloat, and headed for Italy. They floundered for hours as the storm grew worse. Looking desperately around, Caesar saw the Vampyre at the rail looking out over the storm. Taking advantage of this distraction and the raging of the storm, he stumbled across the deck, shouldering the surprised Vampyre into the sea. As he watched the Vampyre being pulled further from the boat by the storm, Caesar wondered if it could be killed; at least it would take some time to get back to the others if it survived. He immediately turned and instructed the captain to turn the boat toward Greece.

As soon as he returned to his camp, he dispatched men with letters to Antony instructing him to bring the rest of the army. Meanwhile, his men begged him to have faith in them and attack the enemy while the Hidden Ones clamored for blood.

After four nerve-racking months of waiting and many rejected attempts at peace, Caesar finally got his reinforcements. They had been stopped by a blockade and forced to bide their time until the opportunity came for their crossing. Winter storms and the starved condition of the blockading fleet eventually allowed them their chance to break through. Caesar, giving in to his fears, believed it more likely that they had been compelled to wait by the Vampyres, who had demanded he fight and, as always, insisted on bloodshed. As soon as the army was reassembled, he intended to rush Dyrrachium, but the wait had been so long that he decided to try a ploy. He had his army set off on a circuitous route to lure Pompey's forces away. Once he felt secure that his opponents must think he was headed elsewhere, he forced his troops into an all-night march on the city.

It seemed to work. He arrived at the city before Pompey could cut him off. Before he could take Dyrrachium, though, Pompey's forces arrived. Julius knew that, numerically, his forces were no match for Pompey, but he decided on a desperate gamble. Using a tactic that had been successful in Gaul, he spread his forces around the opponents. He built fortifications using a smaller army to besiege a larger one, not in the city, but in the open.

The siege dragged on for a time, seeming to be a stalemate. Julius had no way to get new supplies, and Pompey's armies had enough to outlast him. The day came when he saw his chance. Pompey was setting up a new camp to stretch Caesar's line further. So, Julius gathered thirty-three cohorts and split them into two columns of men, intending to catch the new camp by surprise and capture the men. He led one group and sent the other around to approach from the opposite direction. He entered the camp with his men and carried the fight well; however, the other group did not arrive. His men were beaten in a brutal battle, and over a thousand soldiers were lost or captured. He took what dead he could, seeking to keep them from becoming food, but grew disheartened when he learned the captured men had been slaughtered. It was not right to slaughter captives in this fashion, and Julius grew sure that there was more opposing him than Pompey and the fools he had with him. Having grown fearful that some of his standard-bearers were under an evil sway, he decided to withdraw to a more favorable position.

For weeks, they marched around Greece, harried by Pompey's troops. After successfully leading Pompey away from his ships and supplies on the Adriatic, the two men and their armies met on the plains of Pharsalia. The two armies camped opposite each other, but neither general seemed willing to commit to battle. Julius, thinking perhaps Pompey was frightened to face him in open battle, began having his troops drill on the open plains between the armies. *Maybe*, he thought, *Pompey would see the discipline of my troops and realize that he must accept my offers of peace or be destroyed. Surely, he understands we can finish this with no further bloodshed.*

As he prepared for this demonstration, he noticed that the opposition was preparing for battle. So, he rallied his troops and once again exhorted them to conduct themselves with honor. *Kill when necessary, but not when wounding would do. Win the day with as many oppositions left alive as possible and trust in his generosity.*

The armies faced each other across the open field. An eerie silence and uneasy tension filled the air. The advance was sounded, and Julius's army rushed into the fray. The Pompeian forces stood their ground, choosing neither to advance nor to retreat, seemingly content to let the enemy come to them. The battle was joined, and the tide went back and forth all morning; in the early afternoon, Caesar's superior tactics began to win over Pompey's superior numbers. By late afternoon, Pompey had retreated to his camp, but not wanting to give up his momentum, Julius stormed him. By evening, it was finished. Julius had won the day. All that remained was to accept the surrender of the remaining troops. Julius was bitterly disappointed, however, to find that Pompey had, once again, escaped his grasp, having fled during the heat of the battle.

After crushing Pompey's forces at Pharsalia, Caesar was hailed as a hero throughout Greece and Asia. He had merely to march past a city to be given tribute and sworn allegiance. Convinced that another, even more savage group of Vampyres had been behind Pompey's needless waste of life, he spent seven weeks touring the eastern part of the Empire, securing his rule, and scouring for any sign of these other creatures. His "Masters" didn't complain, as there were festivals and offerings in every city they visited. He shuddered every time sacrifices were offered to the gods on his behalf, knowing that, somehow, Vampyres were behind it all and benefiting from every drop of blood spilled.

At last, word came to him that Pompey had turned up in Africa, the last part of the Empire left to him. He was forced to cut his tour of Asia short to end this feud with Pompey and get to the real business at hand. He traveled to Rhodes and set sail for Alexandria, where Pompey was said to have fled.

Chapter 4
October 48 to Spring 47 BC

During the three days it took three days to sail to Egypt, his meeting with Pompey kept playing out in Julius's head. They would meet in Alexandria, where Pompey would no doubt have heard that Caesar was a hero to the rest of the Empire. Pompey would realize the hopelessness of his situation and beg his old friend's forgiveness. Julius would respond by accepting Pompey with open arms and welcoming him into his good graces. Together, they would restore Rome and drive the Vampyres from the Republic, freeing the populace and ensuring the aristocracy could govern Rome properly without the hidden agendas of an evil race.

His mood was such that when he tripped upon stepping ashore, he did not take this as an ill omen. Instead, he laughed and cried out, "Ah, Egypt, I embrace you as you will embrace me." As he stood and dusted himself off, he spotted a group of royal courtiers sent by Ptolemy to welcome him. Surely, this was a good sign; Pompey had made known his intentions to renew his allegiance to Caesar and had even convinced the Egyptian king to send gifts. He prepared to receive them, standing as tall and regal as he could make himself appear, anxious to be done with the formalities and reacquaint himself with his old friend turned enemy.

The Egyptians approached, smiling, and presented him with a box of finely carved ebony, large enough to hold a tidy offering. Caesar nodded, and they opened the box to show him its contents. The Egyptians knelt, and a shrouded figure glided to the box's side. He stared at the creature and the open box; what were Vampyres doing here in Egypt? Was the box and its contents from the Egyptians or the Vampyres? From both? He began to fear what was in the box. Minutes ticked by as he stared at the creature, unable to move. At last, the dark messenger smiled and bent down toward the offering. He held his breath as the creature reached in. It felt like hours but was probably mere moments that the withered hand dallied inside. As tension mounted, it finally straightened and withdrew Pompey's head. From the depth of the creature's cowl came, "A gift from Egypt to you, Caesar. May our two kingdoms enjoy peace."

Caesar was stunned. The world was spinning. He stared in a daze as the head was placed back into the box, the lid was closed, and the box was laid before him. Too appalled to speak, he watched silently as the procession retreated into the city.

Overwhelmed, he collapsed to the ground and wept. His old comrade had been denied the opportunity to repent his selfish actions. Caesar had dared to dream that Pompey would come to his side, hoping that he would gain a companion he could confide in and have a partner in this fight against the Vampyres. He remained alone. Who now could help him conduct the secret war he had been planning? Who would he confide in? Who would share the horrors he had been subjected to?

As Caesar arose, resolution firmed his motions. The Vampyres would answer for this. They could not take all that was dear to him and expect him not to make them pay. He was the greatest general the world had ever known. Once he had delved into their secrets, the Vampyres would be wiped from the earth. Being descended from Venus herself ensured the favor of the gods. Fortune had followed him despite the constant interference of the damned. There would be a day of reckoning, and evil would tremble before him. Donning his consular toga, Julius gathered his escort and entered the city. He would set up residence in the royal palace to remind Egypt it was still allied with Rome and that it was in their best interest to please him lest that allegiance change.

Upon gaining entrance, Julius requisitioned a wing and set up offices. His first order of business was to send for reinforcements. Next, he sent word to Ptolemy and his sister, Cleopatra, that he wished to meet with them and settle their dispute over who governed Egypt. The late king had left the land to his two eldest children, as was the tradition, and somehow, the thirteen-year-old Ptolemy was in control while his twenty-one-year-old sister was in hiding. Julius was sure Vampyres were behind this and was determined to know why.

Late one night, as he was reviewing correspondences from Rome, there came a gentle knock on his door, and a strange old man entered carrying a carpet bag slung over his shoulder.

"I don't know why you were allowed to get this far," Julius said. "It would be in your best interest to see yourself out immediately." At this, the man set his burden gently on the ground and began to unfasten the cinch at the top of the bag. Julius rose in alarm and reached for his sword. Warily, he watched as the man prepared for whatever may happen next. Julius's alarm gave way to awe as the cinch was released, and the bag dropped around its contents. Out of the bag stepped a beautiful young woman. "You must be Cleopatra," he said.

"Yes, my lord," she replied. "I must apologize. This is not how I would have had our first meeting, but I saw no other way." Her voice was soft yet commanding. Even stepping out of a carpet bag in rags, she seemed regal. She projected her presence with assurance beyond her age and seemed in complete control of the situation. This, of course, was absurd given that she was carried in like a peddler's goods and stood before him in rags, yet he knew instantly that this was a woman not to be taken lightly. He immediately felt protective of her.

"Could you not have made an appointment to see me during the day as appropriate?" he asked as he cleared his throat to give himself time to take in the situation and the overwhelming person who stood before him.

"No, my lord. I am afraid I never would have gotten close to the palace had my brother's Magicians known I was coming." Magicians? Did she mean the Vampyres? Perhaps she knew something that would be of more use to him than he had anticipated.

"Surely you do not fear Magicians," he began. "I would not expect such superstition from one who has been so well educated."

Cleopatra dismissed her servant with a wave of her hand. He exited quickly, closing the door silently behind him. "I am not superstitious, my lord, but these Magicians are real. I have seen their power. They use my brother as a puppet. They have taken my kingdom and seek to deny my rights as the eldest in the royal line."

Julius was anxious to discover what she knew but forced himself to proceed cautiously; he never knew what was happening when Vampyres were involved. "Tell me of these Magicians then," he said. "What power do they have, and why do they rob you and seem to give so generously to Ptolemy?"

"He is weaker than I am. They only seem to give to him. He is but a tool for them, something to hold before the people while they carry out their agenda, an agenda that would appear to include you, my lord." She gave away her nervousness with a wobble in her voice and a twitch of her eyes. This would be one of the few times Julius ever saw her lose her composure, lasting no more than a second.

"Really?" he asked. "What would these plans be, and how do you know them?"

"I know only what my spies in the palace can get to me, and that is not much. I know there are places deep under the palace where they would have no one go. I also know that when it was discovered you were on your way to our shores, they grew excited and commanded that your enemy's head be presented to you as a show of their good faith. My advisers counseled me not to come. They said you would be under the sway of their magic, but I know the great Caesar would not bow to such."

Julius was filled with shame. He had done the bidding of the Vampyres for most of his life. He sat behind his desk and looked at her; he knew this would be an important decision. How much could she be trusted? How much did she need to know? "I believe these Magicians are the same creatures I have been fighting my entire life," he began. "So far as I can tell, they have secretly ruled Rome for many years, perhaps from the beginning. They are mysterious and powerful, and I have been searching for their secrets. I do not believe they are human. Perhaps they once were, I do not know." Julius paused, seeking the right words. He must only reveal enough to win her confidence and draw what he could from her. Before he could begin again, a commotion began in the outer rooms. He opened the door to his bed chamber and waved her in. After securing the door behind her, he settled himself at his desk, his sword within easy reach, to wait for whatever was next.

The door flew open, and Ptolemy strode in, flanked by three Vampyres. Julius smiled, not bothering to stand. The young king appeared upset and was on the verge of speaking when one of the Vampyres touched his shoulder and stepped before the boy.

"Welcome to Egypt, Caesar," it said. It spoke Greek with an unknown but heavy accent. "It seems those you represent are the new power in Rome and perhaps the world. Our kind has been kept as advisers in Egypt for far too long. We seek to enrich our status here and share in the glory of Rome. It was expected that your handlers would have spoken to us by now. Was our gift not enough?"

"You do not know what you speak of, Magician," Julius sneered. "Those you speak of are not my handlers. I have no Master."

The Vampyre stepped back in surprise. "Oh?" it said. "I think not. You will ensure they know we desire a meeting. The king is willing to submit to Rome, provided he is made a full citizen and given governorship of all Egypt. Rome will share her glory." All three Vampyres turned as one and exited the room, leaving the boy king to catch up, red-faced and humiliated. Moments after, one door shut and the other opened. Cleopatra stepped out from his bed chamber.

"I believe there is more you have not told me. If you choose to have the future queen of Egypt as an ally, then when we next meet, we will exchange *all* we know. There can be no secrets between such as us, Caesar," Cleopatra stated, and with that, she scooped up her carpet bag and left.

Julius dismissed all his servants from the outer chambers, sat at his desk, and waited. His selection of rooms had been intentional. There was no way in or out except the front door. This could be problematic in an uprising in the palace, but it ensured he would have no unwanted visitors. He settled in, facing the door. They would not be able to catch him off guard this time.

Later, the door opened, and a Vampyre silently entered, seeming to instantly move from the door to the desk. "You have had some visitors," it said. "The girl was here for some time. Was she entertaining?" Caesar stiffened. His protective feelings for Cleopatra already ran deep. Before he could answer, the Vampyre smiled. "That is not important. We have been watching these 'Magicians,' as they call themselves. We are not pleased with them. We, the true Children of The Wolf, rule all other Vampyres. Calling themselves Magicians does not negate this fact. You will not back Ptolemy or his Magicians. These greedy upstarts wish to partake in the spoils of what we have so fastidiously worked for. The glory and benefits of Rome will stay with those who have created them, not be given to beggars who come too late in the game."

Careful to still his features, Caesar paused as if considering his orders. Finally, their aims provided a way for him to have an ally with whom he could plan their downfall. "So, you would like me to back his sister's claim to the throne?" he asked.

"If that pleases you," came the response. "Just ensure your new plaything renders unto Rome what is ours." The Vampyre smirked and turned. It seemed to appear at the door for an instant, then was gone, and the door left open a crack behind it.

Caesar arose from his seat and mechanically moved to the door, shutting it gently, his mind overflowing with possibilities. Ambling around the room, he straightened wall hangings, moved furniture, and paced. *I must be careful*, he thought. *If she knows some things about them that I don't, this alliance has the potential to give me what I need. They must go on believing that my fascination with Cleopatra is nothing more than a distracting dalliance. I cannot give them more things to hurt me with. Plans must be made. I must win her to my side, bring Egypt fully into the Republic, and ensure she rules here. To make these plans, we must be alone. No Vampyres, no servants, or potential spies.*

Days went by with no word from Cleopatra. Caesar could not contact her and was unsure what his next step should be. Once the next step was taken, the rest would fall into place. As he prepared to retire one evening, he felt he was being watched. Glancing around, he saw no one. Eventually, as the feeling persisted, he sat at his desk and waited.

"What is it I can do for you now?" he asked aloud. "Or am I to be watched while I sleep?"

A few seconds later, a Vampyre stepped from the shadows. This was the one, the strange one from Britannia. Something was different. The Vampyre's hood was pushed back, and its features were visible. It moved to the chair opposite Caesar's desk in a deliberate manner. Staring at him the entire time as if deciding his fate, the Vampyre sat, yet it did not speak, only that sad and quizzical stare. Caesar sensed something was amiss and waited for the Vampyre to begin.

"It is ones like you that cause me the most concern, Gaius," it said. "I see in you both the bright hope and the dark horror of humanity. Most humans are helplessly lost, just trying to survive as long as they can in this world. The few exceptions can mostly be lumped into two categories: the selfless hero and the selfish. The selfish may seem benign, but they always manifest their corruption in the end."

"And which am I?" Julius asked. "What does your kind think of me?"

The Vampyre sighed. "My kind? Save for one other, I am alone in this world. But that is for another time." It paused in thought and began again. "What you need to know is what I think of you. You are among the great, those few in humanity with the potential to shape the world. Those few are always enigmatic, brilliant, egotistical, altruistic, and selfish." The Vampyre nodded toward Julius and stared into the depths of his soul. "What remains to be seen is how you will manifest. Will your selfishness and ego win over your love for mankind, or will your affection for your kind stay your ego and self-love, keeping the monster you could become in check?"

Caesar laughed. "You speak of monsters as if you are not one yourself. You accuse me of horrors I have not committed while you drain Rome of blood to sustain your evil plans. Who is the greater enigma?"

"I have much to answer for, young Caesar, and my conscience weighs heavily. My struggle has been long and may never end, but do not confuse me with those who have dominated your life for so long." The Vampyre looked as if it were about to leave, seemed to struggle with a decision, and began again. "Over a millennium ago, I was a mortal man like you, a leader among my people. I have seen many things since that time. The world grows larger, yet it gets smaller at the same time. Those who lead, lead more people and govern more land than ever before. Your actions affect so much more than one small community of tribes. The origins of the Vampyres are my burden, one you need not know. What you need to know is this: they are not magical. They are not immortal, and they can be killed. Their life span is far greater than your own. Their strength, speed, vision, hearing, and sense of smell are beyond your experience. These strengths are also weaknesses." Once again, the Vampyre's voice trailed off. When it spoke again, its whisper was barely audible. "I left my home in Powys, a part of what you call Britannia, to try and bring balance to Rome. Perhaps I thought, after all these years, the Vampyres here were ready to listen and see reason. I now realize I was wrong; the greed and corruption lay as deep as ever. I will return to my home soon and await the time when things can be made right." Once again, that piercing stare burned right through him. "I have given you what you need to help Rome free herself from the bonds of slavery she was founded in. I have never so openly aided man in this struggle. I can only hope that your actions will bear the desired fruit. I will leave you now to use what I have given you as you will. Beware of your dual nature, Julius. Do not let glory and selfishness rule your destiny. Rather, feed your better side and become the hero you were meant to be." The Vampyre rose as if it shouldered a heavy burden and walked slowly from his chambers.

It was a restless night for Caesar. The strange Vampyre had revealed much and claimed it had given him what he needed to free his people of the Vampyres' yoke. What did he know? They lived long, extraordinary lives. This did not help. They were stronger, faster, and, in all ways, superior physically to man. How did this help? What was he missing? Caesar struggled to find the key he had supposedly been given. As dawn broke over the Nile, Caesar began to form a plan.

Chapter 5
Capture

Caesar burst from his chamber, surprising his servants. His strange request surprised them even more. He demanded that his office and bed chamber be fitted with sconces mere inches apart in two rows, midway up the wall, and a torch fitted into each sconce. Furthermore, he desired polished metal to be placed along the lower wall and ceiling. As this was being done, he ordered all pungent herbs and spices from the kitchen in sealed containers and placed them throughout his chambers. He then sent word to Ptolemy that his request for an audience had been denied. He knew the Magicians would get the message and understand it was for them. Before returning to his chambers, Caesar found four of his most trusted men, men of the Tenth Legion who had been with him since Gaul. He explained to them that he intended to capture Ptolemy and his Magicians and that he had learned the secret to counter the Egyptians' magic but needed help. The guards were told no more than they needed to know and sworn to secrecy.

Caesar hid three guards in his bed chamber and left one outside his office door. He then sat at his desk and waited for the Magicians and their puppet to arrive. His sword was within easy reach, and the only light was a lone candle on his desk. He did not have to wait long before he heard Ptolemy outside the door demanding that the guard stand aside and allow the King of Egypt to pass. The guard, as planned, hesitated long enough to further enrage the Egyptians before allowing them in. They stormed into the room as planned and, in anger, failed to notice the changes in the chamber. This gamble would determine if Caesar's guesses were correct. It would be the beginning of his victory or, possibly, the end of his life.

At once, Ptolemy demanded to know the meaning of the denial. Caesar had no right to refuse him an audience with his Masters. Caesar yelled, "Now!" and the guards burst in. One lit a torch, causing each torch in line to catch fire, while two broke open the jars of herbs and spices, shattering the pottery and banging their swords into the polished metal, creating as much clamor as they could. The torches were so close together that, as the first torches were lit, the flames spread rapidly along the two rows, filling the room with light glinting off the polished metal. Even to Caesar and his men, the light was overly bright and the smell so pungent they nearly gagged. As quick as it all was, the Magicians were quicker. Before the guards could intervene, Caesar was dangling by his neck from the grip of an Egyptian Vampyre. He had no leverage with his feet off the ground, and his sword was no longer within reach. But the strangling grip only lasted a few seconds as the din rose in the room along with the light and the overpowering scent. The Vampyres fell to the floor, covering their eyes and ears, groveling in surprise and pain. Their breath came in choked gasps as they struggled to overcome the assault on their senses. Ptolemy stood in shock, unable to respond to the unexpected change of events.

Only two Vampyres had come with Ptolemy, and Caesar and his three men immediately fell upon them. Two of them struggled to subdue one while Caesar and the other man bound the other. Even with all of Caesar's advantages, he was amazed at how difficult it was to wrap the ropes and chains around this creature. Its strength was incredible, and it took longer than expected to bind and gag it. They turned and helped the others with the second Vampyre when the first was bound. Although still disabled by the light and smell in the room, this one was getting over its initial surprise and was fighting back with its eyes clamped shut and holding its breath. They finally managed to bind the creature with chains and rope. Once both creatures were bound, they were placed in carpet bags, which were again wrapped in chains and rope. Only after this was done did they turn their attention to Ptolemy. The boy's regal bearing was gone, and he stood there, a frightened thirteen-year-old out of his element. Swords drawn, the guards surrounded the boy. Caesar picked up his sword and gently placed the tip of it to Ptolemy's throat.

"How many more of them are there?" he demanded.

Ptolemy swallowed, causing his Adam's apple to press against the tip of the sword and draw a drop of blood. "I don't know," he said. "Only my three advisers live in the palace. The others occupy temples as high priests."

"Where is your third adviser, boy?" Caesar growled, raising the sword's tip to the boy's cheek. "How come he is not here?"

Tears trickled from Ptolemy's eyes. "I don't know!" he

sobbed. "I have not seen him since we last were in this room! The others seemed agitated at his disappearance but told me nothing."

Caesar lowered his sword. "You are my prisoner," he said. "You will be confined to your quarters. Your servants and guards will be replaced by my own."

Two of Caesar's guards, dressed in the Magicians' clothes, escorted the boy back to his room. They would not hold up under scrutiny, but casual observers would believe the boy and his Magicians had come and gone without incident. With his immediate goals accomplished, Caesar sent some servants to remove the metal and sconces while others scrubbed the floors to remove the scent of the herbs. He placed the two Vampyres in locked chests in his sleeping quarters. Word soon spread that the boy king was captive, and Rome backed Cleopatra's claim.

That evening, he had two visitors. The first was Cleopatra. She entered dressed in her royal best, far from the bag and rags of their last meeting.

"I see you have made a decision." Cutting her off, Caesar motioned her to silence. Locking the door to the outer chambers, he led her into the bedroom and locked that door. "What is it you have in mind?" she asked, raising her eyebrows. Once again, Caesar motioned for her to be silent. He walked over to one of the chests, unlocked its lid, and opened it with a smile.

"A surprise I think you will enjoy, my dear. Behold." Caesar reached into the chest and pulled up the chain-wrapped carpet bag. "An idea I got from you," he said as he untied the top and lowered it enough to unveil the gagged face of the Magician it contained. The creature stared at them both. Fear and anger registered on its face, and it struggled with its bonds. Caesar pulled the bag back over its head, retied the top, and pushed the creature back down in the iron-bound box, locking the lid over it again.

"I am impressed," Cleopatra said. "I would not have thought it possible to capture them alive. But what of those you serve? Are they any better than these?"

Caesar took her back into the office chamber and told her the whole story. For hours, he explained how he had met them and how they had ruled and ruined his life ever since. He told her he planned to destroy them, and about the strange one from Britannia and the information it had given him. When he was done, he invited her to join him in the coming war to free Rome from these creatures forever. "We would have to keep this a secret from the people," he said. "We cannot afford to panic the populace. We would also have to continue to pretend to do their bidding until we are ready to strike. Egypt will become officially a province of Rome. If we do not do this, we will both lose our lives, and puppets will take our places, only too happy to do their bidding through fear or for personal gain."

She considered what he had said. After several minutes of contemplation, she looked up at him. "I see no other choice for Egypt or Rome," she said. "My brother is as much a victim of these creatures as you or anyone else. We will be united in this, but I want him protected until we discern if he was simply under their sway or welcomed their support in ousting me."

"Agreed." said Caesar. "We will not harm any pawns unless they are of evil intent themselves, or it cannot be avoided. For now, we will keep the pretense of a romance between you and me. It supplies an adequate reason for us to be alone, thus not arousing suspicion." When Cleopatra left, she had been in his chambers for several hours, long enough to start rumors of a budding romance throughout the palace.

Soon, his second visitor arrived. "You have had a very busy day," it said. "Servants bustling about all morning, a visit from the upstarts announcing your support for Cleopatra, and a few hours behind closed doors?" It smirked at Caesar while it spoke. "Tell me of the visit from Ptolemy. We see you have placed him under arrest. What of his Magicians? Any trouble with them? Tell me, why does it stink so in your chambers today?"

"I sent word to Ptolemy this morning that his request for an audience with you had been denied," Caesar began his well-rehearsed lie. "He came with two of his Magicians. I told them that you had decided it was in the best interest of Rome to back Cleopatra and that no Egyptian, Magician or otherwise, had any rights to the glory of Rome. They became enraged and broke open several jars of herbs stored temporarily in this chamber. Shortly after that, they left with no explanation. It was strange; I had feared they would kill me or attempt to extract some sort of revenge. Instead, shortly after their violent outburst, they fled with Ptolemy in tow. I sent servants and guards to secure him in his chambers and, again, was met with no resistance. I have not seen them since."

It's no wonder," the Vampyre laughed. "I can only imagine the stench in this room if it still smells so now."

"Really?" asked Caesar innocently. "I cannot smell anything now. Perhaps I have become accustomed to it."

The Vampyre's smile vanished as if realizing too late that it had said too much. "Strange how the nose becomes accustomed to such things," it said. "You need not worry about these Magicians. We have been interviewing one of them for the past few days. Their numbers are few; we will take care of them. As for the other two advisers, we will find them. Do not concern yourself." It grinned again and continued. "Enjoy your plaything. Just make sure you secure Egypt for us. We will soon have more to do. Do not dally overlong here." Having said all it came to say, it vanished.

Caesar smiled at its departure. He now had a measure of their strength. He knew their senses could be overpowered, crippling them, and was beginning to understand how to watch them despite their incredible speed. Doors still needed to be opened, curtains moved. Their passing stirred candles. Yes, they could be defeated. Now, he needed answers to new questions. How many of them were there? Where else were they if they were in Rome, Britannia, and Egypt? They had said their number in Egypt was few compared to Rome. Did this mean ten in Egypt? 100 in Rome? Or 100 in Egypt and thousands in Rome? Yes, he decided, that is the next question that must be answered. How many of the enemy existed and where? Fortunately, he had two captives who just might be persuaded to answer questions.

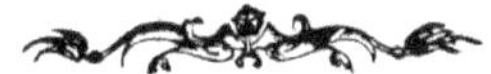

As soon as word spread that Rome was backing Cleopatra and claiming Egypt, Ptolemy's military commanders and the remaining Vampyres in Egypt began to stir the populace in Ptolemy's name. It was not yet known that he was captive in his own palace. The palace was stormed by soldiers loyal to Ptolemy who claimed they did so at his command. Caesar's reinforcements had yet to arrive, and he was hard-pressed to hold back the insurgents. After several assaults on the palace, Caesar held a public meeting. He had to convince the people they were mistaken and that Rome and Egypt were partners until more troops came. He appeared with Cleopatra at his side and explained that Cleopatra and Ptolemy were to be co-rulers in accordance with the wishes of the old king. He even went so far as to promise Cyprus would be returned to Egypt so that Cleopatra's two youngest siblings could have it to rule, and all would be as was dictated by Cleopatra's father before he died. This did little to sway the populace as the high priests and commanders loyal to Ptolemy's cause continued to foment rebellion. There were continued assaults on the palace, and Caesar began to worry that all would be lost if his reinforcements did not arrive soon.

The atmosphere in the palace was tense. The troops and servants were concerned that the ships in the harbor controlled by Ptolemy would cut them off from re-supply by sea. Several of the wells had been poisoned, and Cleopatra was concerned that they could not continue to hold off the assaults on the palace. Julius could not console Cleopatra and felt on the brink of losing everything. He knew it was time to act. His life had been full of desperate gambles and fortune had always favored him. First, he commanded that new wells be dug. Then, he set about preparing for action. He needed to prove to Cleopatra that they could win and that her faith in him was not misplaced.

Caesar gathered half of his men and briefed them on his plans. It was a desperate gamble, but if they thought it was insane, they kept it to themselves. Caesar's reputation for good fortune was well known, and if anyone could succeed against such odds, it would be him.

In the gray before dawn, they set out from the palace, made their way to the harbor, and set fire to the Egyptian ships there, thus ensuring they would not be cut off from supplies or reinforcements. As the flames spread throughout the ships, the wind began to pick up, and the city's granaries and the famed royal library were soon in flames. The Egyptian army was now alerted to Caesar's movements, and time was of the essence. Taking advantage of the distraction of the fire, Caesar's engineers began to erect a bridge to the island and a lighthouse offshore. He intended to control the harbor. He and his men rowed out to take the island. As he began his assault, the defenders, distracted by the flames from the mainland, were taken by surprise. The fight was going well. His men were in such good spirits that even the oarsmen wanted to get in on the action and scurried ashore, hurling stones and slinging insults at the Egyptian soldiers. This breach of discipline worried Caesar, but things were well in hand, and he thought to correct it later after the fight.

To his dismay, however, the Egyptians saw their chance and charged the oarsmen. Weaponless and vulnerable, they scrambled back to their ships and attempted to get back to the relative safety of the water. The rest of the Roman soldiers panicked. Shouts went out that the oarsmen were leaving them behind, and a mad dash for the ships ensued. Several ships were swamped and sunk as too many tried to pile in, and several, including Caesar's own, were firmly grounded and could not be cast off. All attempts at rallying the men to return to the fight were useless. Realizing that his situation was untenable, Caesar cast off his commander's cloak, dropped his sword and all that would weigh him down, and swam for safety. His last glimpse as he climbed into a boat and they struck off for shore was of the enemy waving his cloak around like a souvenir, jeering at the fleeing Romans. This was not the decisive victory he had been looking for. Still, they destroyed the Egyptian fleet and showed the enemy that they were not helplessly trapped in the palace.

By now, word had spread that Ptolemy was a captive in the palace. After the fires had been put out, it was discovered that several of the high priests who had been instigating the violence were missing. People began to wonder if they had abandoned them; they started questioning what they were being told and demanded to see Ptolemy. When their demands reached Caesar's ears, he and Cleopatra set off to see the boy in his chambers.

"It was a foolish thing you attempted, Caesar," she said. "You could have lost a lot more men than you did or been killed yourself."

"Just look at the results!" he replied. "Their armies are crippled, their soldiers unsure, and it seems the Roman Vampyres may have been out hunting Egyptian ones, as well. We couldn't ask for anything better than them fighting among themselves."

Cleopatra nodded. "Now they want Ptolemy back. He isn't going to want to go. He is a new person and so much happier without his advisers."

"This may be just what we need. If the Magicians' numbers have been thinned by the Vampyres and the armies are looking for leadership, maybe releasing him will end this."

Cleopatra laughed. "For a brilliant man, Caesar, you are an unbelievable optimist. You always assume things will just fall into place in your favor."

"I am seldom wrong, my dear. They say I am favored by the gods."

They reached Ptolemy's chambers, nodded to the guards at the entrance, and went inside. The boy was perched on a stool reading a papyrus scroll. "Ah, my sister and my savior! What brings you two here today? Are we to chat some more about ethics and the influence of bad men?" he chuckled. "I believe I have learned that lesson now."

We are here to discuss your release," Caesar said. "The armies and the people would like you returned to them."

Ptolemy paled. "Don't make me go back to them." He began to tremble. "You have no idea what they are like, what they can do."

Caesar sighed. "You must be strong, Ptolemy. Your people need to be told to listen to reason. Bring them into the fold before my reinforcements come." Caesar stopped himself; he didn't want this to sound like a threat. "Go to your generals. Tell them you wish to speak to the people. Let it be known you don't want to see any advisers except the generals. This will flatter them, and they will keep the Magicians away from you."

Ptolemy began to weep. "You don't understand, Caesar. I can't do it! They will find me! They will make me do things!"

Caesar grew impatient with this whining. "Grow up, Ptolemy," he spat. "Do what is right for your people. These Magicians will continue to stir rebellion and unrest if you do not. People will die, boy, and it will be on your shoulders."

Cleopatra glared at Caesar, angry at what he had said but understanding the need to say it. Bloodshed was what the Magicians and Vampyres alike wanted. Only evil would benefit. "It is all right, Ptolemy," she said. "Caesar is right. This is our best chance to prevent further bloodshed."

Ptolemy dried his eyes and stood. He squared his shoulders as best he could and tried to look brave. "As you say, sister," he said. "I can see you will not listen to me, and the decision has already been made." He shrugged as if accepting his fate. "I will leave this afternoon." He turned his back to them and began rolling papyrus scrolls and stuffing them into protective tubes. Cleopatra and Caesar left him to prepare for his departure.

"I don't like this, Julius," she said. "What if he is right and they control him again?" Caesar frowned at that. "What if he is pretending, saying only what we want to hear, and he will welcome them? What if he goes out there, turns the people to our side, and abdicates the throne to you?

Julius shook his head. "No, we will not second guess ourselves. This is the best course of action, and it is done." Once again, Cleopatra only nodded in response. Caesar was right, but she still didn't like it. She had a bad feeling about this. "We did not get enough information from our captives before they died," Caesar said. "The months we have been cooped up here waiting for more of my troops should have been more productive than they were."

"We need to capture a Roman Vampyre," Cleopatra replied, "and we need to find a place to interrogate him without the constant fear of being caught."

Caesar looked at her. "Do you have something in mind?" he asked. "This will be far riskier than before, and we still need to find a way to keep it alive."

They had learned from the captive Magicians that Vampyres did not eat food; they found their sustenance only in human blood. But they had been unwilling to sacrifice people to these things to keep them alive, and within a week, their captives became weak. After thirty days, they began to die. It took much longer for their lives to at last come to an end, but end they did. While useful, this information would hardly win them any battles. It would be impossible to starve them out. The monsters hadn't spoken at all unless it was to issue threats. They were too sure they would be rescued or that Caesar would be caught by the Roman Vampyres and killed. It wasn't until they were too weak to talk that they realized the truth of their situation.

That afternoon, Ptolemy left the palace without a word or a backward glance. Within hours, he was at the head of his army, ready to fight for his right to the throne. It was a sad day for Cleopatra, who believed she had put him back into the clutches of the Magicians. However, Caesar believed they had been played for fools, and Ptolemy was a better schemer than previously suspected.

Chapter 6
Late Spring to Summer 47 BC

Marching overland from Syria was an army of non-Roman citizens of the Republic led by Mithridates of Pergamum. Mithridates was a Cimmerian prince who hoped Caesar's support would enable him to become king of the Bosporan Kingdom under Roman rule. This large outside force must have frightened Ptolemy and his advisers because they immediately sent the bulk of their forces to fight on this new front. Caesar followed by sea and Ptolemy's army was soon beset on both sides, driving them toward the Nile. As this was happening, it was found that Mithridates's army contained at least three thousand Jews. Upon hearing this, the Jewish population of Alexandria rose in support of Caesar. As a result, the enemy was swiftly and thoroughly routed. Ptolemy fled on a boat across the Nile, but his boat was swamped, and he died in the river. Ptolemy's passing was heart-wrenching for Cleopatra, who still believed him a puppet of the Magicians; she felt lost and angry. She was furious with Caesar for letting this happen, but it firmed her hatred of them and her resolve to fight. In the end, she forgave Caesar and focused on their mutual goal.

Seizing this opportunity, Caesar rode into the enemy-held part of Alexandria and took prisoner Ptolemy and Cleopatra's young siblings, Arsinoe and Ptolemy XIV, to prevent further rebellion.

With Cleopatra now firmly in charge of Egypt, she presented a plan to Caesar: they would take a river cruise up the Nile. On the water, they would capture and interrogate a Vampyre. Caesar had no faith in this plan and knew that he needed to get back to Rome, but with the depth of her grief over her brother and the strength of her hatred of the Vampyres, he found he did not have the heart to deny her.

The queen had a special barge outfitted for their needs. It was reinforced with timbers and double-hulled so that it would not easily sink or be broken into or escaped from. She let it be known that this was to ensure their privacy on the water. More than forty crafts in all would make up the flotilla.

On the morning of their departure, Caesar was interrupted by a Vampyre informing him that the trip would not be tolerated. They had learned that their lands to the east were in rebellion and that Marc Antony was showing himself to be an inept ruler in Rome; there was civil unrest that must be dealt with. Caesar simply smiled, stepped into the bright sunlight, and then went to the boat prepared for him. They cast off and were soon headed upriver. He was concerned. This unrest throughout the Republic was not good. It would cause more deaths for the Vampyres to feed on and distract him from his goal of ridding the world of their menace. He was unsure if this trip was wise; they may not capture a Vampyre. If they did, they might not get the information they needed. The only certain thing was that he was needed elsewhere.

That evening, Caesar stood on the deck as the sun set. As the moon came up, the stillness of the night was broken only by the sounds of the river and the light from the other vessels. Before long, he noticed a shadow flicker to his left. He smiled; it was working. They would come to him. He waited, tense and listening, his hand on his sword, but nothing came. Then, he heard the hatch to the cabin squeak, and a muffled scream came from within. Jumping into action, he leaped into the cabin, slamming the door shut behind him, causing the bar to slam down, holding the door fast. In front of him, he saw Cleopatra dangling from the claw of a Vampyre, its long, grotesque fingernails drawing blood from her tender throat.

"Put her down!" he demanded. Still holding Cleopatra in the air, the creature turned slowly to eye Caesar.

"As a result of your insolence, your plaything will die," it growled, "and you will suffer."

Caesar grabbed some bottles carefully placed around the cabin. He hurled them at the Vampyre. As they broke open, they spilled oil saturated in garlic and hot spices all over the thing's face. It dropped Cleopatra and clutched its eyes. The spices in those bottles would burn the eyes of any normal man; Caesar hoped it was far more intense for this creature. As it dropped Cleopatra, Caesar was again in motion, pulling open the shades on the lamps hanging in the cabin. Just as the creature began to recover from the sting in its eyes, the light blinded it, and Cleopatra was on her feet, a rattling sistrum in each hand, waving her arms in and out of the creature's vision, attempting to disorient it further. Caesar tackled it with a blanket, wrapping his legs and arms around it.

Additionally, he screamed as loudly as he could into its ear. While this happened, Cleopatra bound its feet with rope, wrapping and tying the rope up its legs. After she knotted the rope about its knees, it threw Caesar off and reached for Cleopatra. Prepared for this, she tossed more of the pepper in its face, grabbed the sistra, and began screaming again, making as much noise and commotion as possible. Caesar recovered himself and threw his body on the creature from behind, this time knocking it to its face while holding its arms behind its back. Cleopatra slipped a noose on at the elbows and tightened it with all her strength. As she was doing this, Caesar let go of the hand and helped pull the rope tight and slip it through a knot at its feet. Again, pulling with all their strength combined, they could barely get the rope to pull its feet up and arms back. Eventually, they got a rope around its neck and again bound that to its feet. While it struggled, trying to burst out of the ropes, chain lengths were wrapped around it and secured in place. The job was done. Caesar and Cleopatra extinguished the majority of the lanterns and opened the hatch. Leaving the bound Vampyre in the cabin, they stumbled onto the deck and into the cool night air.

They spent the rest of the night on the deck, letting the pungent smells dissipate from the cabin. When the sun rose and light reflected off the river, they commanded that the flotilla anchor. None of the other boats were to be anywhere near their barge. They were in an area of the Nile that was particularly infested with crocodiles, and they hoped that the water and crocs would provide them a measure of safety from the other Vampyres. Nevertheless, as night drew near again, they hung several lit lanterns around the deck and lit several more in the cabin when they finally entered.

The creature was much more subdued. It looked like

it had struggled all night and most of the day against its binds. Just to be sure, they inspected and tightened its chains, then, as before, covered all but its face in a strong sack, tying it tightly around the creature's neck. This done, they propped it up against the bulkhead and began questioning it. How many were there? What did they want? Did they have a single leader? No amount of questions and no amount of torture seemed to have any effect, and they were unable to get it to talk. Therefore, they bound it in a trunk and locked the lid.

For several days, they journeyed up the river, discussing strategies and ideas and sharing any information they had on the nature of the beasts. After the tenth day, they again opened the chest and sat the creature up. It was apparent that it was weak and growing frightened. Holding a lamp to its face, they again questioned it to no avail. Back in the trunk it went for another ten days.

Meanwhile, the flotilla had reached its upriver destination and began the trip back. Cleopatra commanded that the return be slowed and that they anchor in the worst parts of the river. This created great hardship among her guards and cost them many slaves to accomplish, but it was done.

On the thirtieth day, the creature finally spoke. "Blood," it begged. Caesar cut his palm and allowed a small amount of blood to drip into its mouth. Almost immediately, it looked just a bit healthier and further from death. "More!" it demanded.

"Not until you answer some questions," Caesar replied. It made no sound but glared at him with hatred. Holding his cut hand near the Vampyre, Caesar asked again, "How many of you are there?"

After a long pause, it replied, "If all the Vampyres in

the Empire were to come together in one place, we might number half the population of Rome."

This caused Caesar to fall back and land hard on the deck. Rome had hundreds of thousands of voting citizens, accounting for only for the tax-paying, land-owning males. The total population of the city surely approached a million. Even if the Vampyre was exaggerating, this was an unfathomable number of monsters. After he recovered from his shock, he dripped a few more drops in the creature's mouth and asked more questions. Eventually, he learned they could be drowned, though it would take days of being submerged for death to occur. They could be killed by removing the head and by destroying the heart. There were different strengths and abilities among them, the oldest being the strongest. A Vampyre from Britain had been the oldest and most powerful they had ever seen, but it had vanished some months ago.

When, at last, they believed that they had all they would get from this creature, they stabbed it through the heart and cut off its head. They locked the heavy trunk, dragged it topside, and tossed it in the river. Caesar wished he could have kept it alive, hoping for more information, but he had to move on, and setting it free was not an option.

After forty days, they returned to Alexandria, and Caesar prepared to leave. He had to return to govern Rome, and she to govern Egypt. They would restore order and develop ways to hunt the Vampyres. Given the vast numbers of the creatures, they must each recruit trusted people into the cause.

As soon as he was alone, he found himself facing half a dozen or so angry Vampyres. "Where have you been? Where is Carolus?" they demanded.

"I went on a river cruise with my love," Caesar said. "I did not make it a secret what I was doing."

"Carolus was to tell you not to go," they spat. "Where is he?"

"I have no idea who this Carolus is," he said. "Why didn't you send one of your own to talk to me instead of another human servant? He probably just ran away."

"He *is* one of us, you insolent worm!"

"Oh, I didn't know your kind had names." The backhand caught him on the jaw and sent him spinning to the floor, dazed. By the time he had his wits back, the Vampyres were gone.

On the return trip, he was constantly questioned about this missing Carolus and his time on the river. He could tell they no longer trusted him but also that he had become an integral part of their plans, so they could not dispose of him. He landed in Brindisi and began to make his way to Rome. He was reunited with Cicero on the road. He had been unsure if the Senator would ever speak with him again after refusing to support him on his first trip from Brindisi to Rome. He smiled at the man and greeted him with an embrace. "It is good to see you," he exclaimed.

"I must admit, I was worried if you would be so," Cicero said. "Our last meeting did not go well, and I have been given considerable political authority in your absence."

"All is forgiven. Now, we must discuss appointments for the good of Rome." Caesar then outlined the people he wished to be appointed magistrates and praetors. Of course, these people had supported him since Gaul; he needed more allies in high places to maintain his reputation for fierce friendship and generosity. This would both reward his friends and provide him with much-needed stability.

Upon his return to Rome, he found the city in disarray; street gangs ruled, and people regularly stormed the markets to steal food. He searched out Marc Antony and found him drowning in drink.

"What have you done to our city?" Caesar demanded through a clenched jaw. Drunken Antony babbled about not wanting to be a politician and blamed Caesar for forcing him into this situation. Caesar demanded, "Why are troops in the city? Why are they killing innocent women and children?"

"They rebelled. They were storming the markets, causing all kinds of problems. I handled them the only way I knew how! If you wanted it done differently, you should have sent a politician in your stead, not a soldier, or come back yourself," Antony replied.

Sighing with a sudden realization, Caesar looked with sorrow into his friend's eyes. "You're right," he said. "I chose you because I trusted you and my love for you. I should have known this was not the right place for you." Then, with a little of the heat back in his voice, he added, "Still, you should have known better than to beat and murder starving people. When people are starving, you feed them." He turned on his heels and slowly walked away from the sobbing Marc Antony. He had just broken his friend's heart, but it would heal, and Antony would be better for it.

He soon got distribution channels running and again limited interest rates and rent amounts to alleviate the suffering of the poor. He also confiscated the lands of Pompey and his primary supporters, to be auctioned off and used to pay the enormous debts he had incurred during the war. He also encouraged larger towns to "loan" him money to pay his debts, though they realized these loans would never be repaid in a timely manner.

He owed many people debts of gratitude for their support, as well as land and income to the troops that had been with him for so long. Sulla and Pompey had just taken lands from others and given them to their supporters when they took over; Caesar was determined to be different. Instead, he offered publicly held lands and lands in new territories such as Gaul. He offered his supporters the first bid on the confiscated lands of the Pompeians.

As order was restored, debts paid, and new funds acquired, he also began to test Marc Antony, Marcus Brutus, and his nephew, Octavius Julius Caesar, to see if he could bring them into the fold. These were his most trusted and loved allies; he would do well if they were at his side. He wanted to stay longer but had to put down the rest of the unrest, starting with the remaining Pompeians in Africa. He left Marcus Lepidus in charge of Rome with the newly empowered Senate, appointed himself consul for the third time, and again abdicated his dictatorship. He gathered armies and marched to Lilybaeum in Sicily, where he took a fleet to Africa. It was winter, and the seas were not easily sailed. His ships became scattered, and he landed in Africa with a small portion of his fleet. Luckily, the Pompeians were not expecting him to leave Rome so soon, nor did they expect he would attempt a winter crossing. He could remain where they landed while waiting for the rest of his fleet to be found. When the fleet was gathered and they disembarked, he sent the ships back to Sicily for more reinforcements.

During this time, the Vampyres commanded him to gather quickly and strike, to win quickly in Africa and get the larger part of the Republic (or the "herd," as they often called the humans) under control. While he waited for reinforcements to reach him in Tunisia, his men worked on making spears, slings, and all manner of weapons. He could not explain why he had them focus on things that could be thrust through the heart, and he could not let his "Masters" know that this was by design. His men also foraged and met with occasional skirmishes with the enemy. Through it all, he was cheerful and exuberant. He trained men and was often seen among the troops, raising morale and instructing battle tactics. His secret was that a contingent of Vampyres had come with him intending to help make short work of the African problem. He secretly prepared his men to destroy them; he did not intend for any Vampyres to make it out of Africa.

Soon, he got word that some of the enemies coming to meet him had turned back after having their lands attacked while they were gone. This, the Vampyres said, was their doing. *Good*, Caesar thought, *I want them confident and unsuspecting.*

Caesar got some reinforcements and moved to Ruspina to set up his main camp. Word began to spread of Caesar, constantly escaping the larger, better-trained enemy and returning to fight again. His name was already known here as his late uncle was a local hero. Soon, people began to defect to his cause, swelling his ranks and lowering the numbers of the Pompeians. Such did the campaign go until the 6th of April. Caesar's army came to Thapsus and arrayed for battle.

As he was preparing to lead the fight, he was pulled into a tent and beaten by several of the Vampyres. "We know what you are up to, Caesar! You will not succeed! You are finished now!" They left and headed toward the front lines. Before passing out, he got one of his centurions dressed in battle regalia and sent him in his stead. Upon seeing "Caesar" ride out with the troops, the Vampyres instigated the charge, and the battle began without orders from anyone. Caesar's body double yelled a battle cry and joined in the fray. The Vampyres were ruthless warriors; enemy soldiers who attempted to give up were slaughtered. Their bloodthirsty savageness quickly spread among the troops, and the battle became a merciless massacre. As the battle ended, those men that Caesar had specially trained turned and fell upon the Vampyres, yelling that they were instigators. They caught the Vampyres by surprise, and the frenzied troops joined in. The Vampyres were completely overwhelmed. Already weakened after a long battle in the bright sun, they soon fell to Caesar's men. Ultimately, every last Vampyre on the battlefield fell to Caesar's men. The battle had been so brutal and pitiless that no one could recall who had turned on the "instigators" or even what they had instigated. However, there was no doubt in his army's mind that a great victory had been won that day.

When they heard about Caesar's triumph at Thapsus, the remaining Pompeians laid down their arms and took ships back to Italy. The leader of the remaining armies, seeing himself abandoned by his men, took his own life.

Chapter 7
March 46 to 15 March 44 BC, The Ides of March

Caesar soon left for Namibia, and when it was discovered that Caesar's army was approaching, King Juba took his own life rather than face such an enemy. Caesar carved out the province of Africa Nova, quickly set it in order, and assigned a governor. While there, he met with the kings and queens of neighboring nations, all of whom had been in contact with Cleopatra and were anxious to help in his fight. He left some of his select troops behind to help train the special armies of these new allies. His confidence was high, and he was sure of his victory. He dispatched armies to Spain to deal with two of Pompey's sons who were stirring some rebellion and then headed for Rome. At last, the civil war was over. He could finally get down to the task at hand.

He entered Rome in a white chariot pulled by a white horse. He was met by Marc Antony and Marcus Brutus and greeted them warmly. "Let us enjoy our reunion!" he cried, and he took the time to do so. He immediately threw a forty-day celebration of his victory. There were gladiators, games, and food. The mood in Rome was at an all-time high, and the people praised his name. As this was happening, he conferred with Antony and Brutus to discover what had transpired in his absence. They reported that some Vampyres had been recruiting Senators and spreading rumors that Caesar was planning to end the Republic and become king. *Good*, he thought, *they are scared. Vulnerable. We can destroy them.*

He called a meeting of the Senate. As he entered, they cheered and declared him a hero of Rome and made him dictator for ten years to re-establish the government now that the war was over. Surprised, Caesar accepted, thinking of the leeway it would give him to fight the Vampyres further. This move, however, nourished a seed of doubt that had been in Brutus's mind. Were the other Senators right? Was Caesar gearing up to proclaim himself king? He never expressed these doubts. Caesar, Antony, Brutus, and Octavius used the forty-day diversion to gather some of the armies' best and most loyal veterans. They brought them into their confidence and taught them about Vampyre hunting.

The Vampyres continued to approach Caesar, and he appeased them as much as possible. They had noted that the ones who left for Africa never came home, which did not sit well with them. They also complained that he subtly modified many of their orders and ignored some others. They were displeased. They began to work harder on the Senators. But such was Caesar's popularity among the people and certain members of the Senate, they had difficulty turning the Senate against him and didn't want to end him until they had another puppet. Knowing his time was limited and desiring to liberate Rome, Caesar sent Marc Antony to Cleopatra. He was to explain the situation and determine how the war was going in Egypt and Africa.

Meanwhile, Caesar's special forces were busy hunting in the twilight, when the Vampyres were most likely to be lurking in the streets, but the light and noise of the city were still present enough to be distracting. One by one, they were hunting and destroying the enemy. This also did not go unnoticed.

The Vampyres began to develop a plan to get rid of Julius Caesar. They picked away at Brutus's doubts and fears. If all went well, he would be their next puppet. They had Senators in their sway begin to work on him, whispering about Caesar's ambitions and the danger he represented. Loyal to Caesar but unsure of his aspirations, Brutus grew ever more trepidatious.

During his fight against the Vampyres, Caesar continued to enact social and political reform. He added more magistrates and court officials, additional priests, and new temples. He was widening the size of the government to make it less susceptible to external influences. He also decreed that a portion of all farm workers be free men, and he attempted to alleviate the suffering of the slaves. He even implemented a new calendar. To spite the mostly nocturnal Vampyres, he abolished the lunar calendar and implemented one based on the solar year. He would make the year's twelve lunar months more evenly numbered, changing the year from 355 days to 365 days. The message was that the Romans would no longer be subject to the night.

In response to his slights, his former Masters were now officially his enemies. They fomented rebellion in Spain, convincing the heirs of Pompey that they were due a leading role in the government. Once again, the Pompeian flag was raised against him. He quickly gathered armies about him and set off for Spain. He traveled fast and, having been down this road before, had almost immediate success. He had great momentum and the enemy was falling into his hands. He was feeling unbeatable when he came to the town of Munda. It was there, he discovered, that the Vampyres intended to end his campaign. Nearly every tenth soldier lined up against him was a bloodsucker.

Additionally, Caesar would be fighting uphill against superior numbers. Any sane assessment of the situation had him withdrawing and fighting when the battlefield was not so stacked against him, but Caesar had had enough. Fueled by his hatred of the Vampyres, exasperation with Pompey's progeny, and tiredness of war, he sounded the charge. Many of the men he had with him were trained in the new fighting style—always go for the heart or the neck. At the first clash, many Vampyres and Pompeians were surprised to find themselves skewered through the heart on the end of a spear. An inordinate number of heads were severed from shoulders, and Caesar was emboldened. Before long, though, the enemy's greater numbers and more advantageous positions, not to mention the Vampyres, began to turn the tide of the battle. Caesar's men, faced with almost certain defeat, began to retreat.

When he saw this, he grabbed a shield and pushed to the front of the ranks. He began berating his men. "Look!" he called. "Your old commander is not afraid!" He was left alone with arrows raining down upon him. Shield raised, he heckled the retreating men. "See! I am unharmed! If you leave me here, I will win this battle alone! Imagine the shame you will feel knowing you left me to such whelps as these!" Whether emboldened or embarrassed, he did not know, but his army charged back into the fray and rejoined the battle.

Just like before, though, the tide quickly turned against them. Determined to defeat this enemy or die, Caesar fought on at the front, and his men rallied around him. Just when he thought his end was at last at hand, a large portion of the enemy suddenly turned and fled. Something was coming at them from the rear. As the flanking army approached, he recognized their dress and fighting style. It was the armies of the African kingdoms that his men had been training to fight Vampyres. They had received word that the Vampyres were forming an army in Spain and were determined to stop them. This timely intervention saved Caesar and the few men he had left. He suffered huge losses in this battle. Pompey's sons had fled, but Caesar sent troops to find them; they would not be able to rebel again. Before leaving the scene, he and his allies found all the dead Vampyres and placed their heads on pikes. Caesar was now in open war with them.

Before returning to Rome, Caesar ensured that Spain and Gaul were properly in hand. He could ill afford any more distractions. While traveling the country freeing slaves and giving Roman citizenship, he received a messenger that came bearing the heads of the last of Pompey's line.

When, at last, the job of ensuring proper government in the provinces was done, he returned to Rome. He knew what he was going to face there. In his absence, he had received word that both Cicero and Brutus had written books extolling the virtues of Cato, a rebel who had taken his own life in Africa. These books painted Caesar as a petty tyrant. He knew Vampyres were urging the Senate to rise against him, and he knew the people were tired of these constant wars. He was losing control. Cicero and Brutus's books had wounded him deeply. He felt abandoned and alone.

Frustrated with the duplicitous nature of his friends and knowing he would soon lose public support for the war, he desperately determined that he would bring the fight to the Vampyres once and for all. He would end this threat or die; either way, he would no longer be tossed about on the stormy sea of his political ambitions. Cleopatra's growing network of spies had sent word that the seat of Vampyre power was to the east in the Parthian Empire. He resolved to attack them there, breaking their hold on his people for good.

After returning to Rome, his mood was foul. He attempted to be genial and gregarious; perhaps he even succeeded occasionally, but the difference was obvious. He was distracted and reticent. He set about ordering the Republic before leaving for the Parthian war. He granted holdings and benefits to veterans, set forth years' worth of building projects, and outlined a future that would decrease unemployment and raise the standard of living for the common man. He ignored the aristocracy, declared himself dictator for life, and made arrangements for Marc Antony and Octavian to be his heirs. All his lands and wealth would go to them. This would also give them considerable political power. He determined that he would leave for the Parthian war in April.

His mood, the laws he dictated without informing the Senate, and most of all, the seemingly mad move of declaring himself dictator for life gave the Roman Vampyres all the leverage they needed to win over key members of the Senate, including Brutus. On some level, Caesar knew this, but his obsession with freeing himself and Rome of the Vampyres consumed his mind. He was leaving the insanity of political life for the straightforward life of a general at war. He would either return victorious, thus having the power to be untouchable, or he would die killing Vampyres. Either way, he could not sit around Rome anymore. Distracted by his preparations for war, he didn't think anything odd when the Senate asked him to come to a closed session on the Ides of March. He barely even noticed the guards now stationed outside the doors when he entered, and he did not hear Marc Antony and Octavius calling to him not to go in. The doors closed around him, and he was immediately beset by Senators asking for favors or clarifications or any number of things in the guise of governing in his absence. In all the tumult, twenty-two Senators stabbed Caesar, and as he lay dying, Brutus came forth and took the killing blow. The last thing Julius heard was his former friend and confidant whisper, "I would rather deal with them than you."

Seven hundred years ago, Rome had begun as a kingdom ruled by Vampyres. The last king of Rome had been a vile tyrant, 500 years ago, a man named Brutus had cast him from the city and established the free Republic, moving the Vampyres to the shadows. Now Rome was to become an Empire; and a man named Brutus had delivered the death blow to the free Republic and took a huge step toward restoring the iron-fisted rule of the Vampyres.

Epilogue

After Caesar's assassination, the Vampyres attempted to use Brutus to form their desired Empire. For a time, Vampyres were more prevalent in society. However, Octavian, Marc Antony, and Marcus Lepidus led Caesar's special forces and other troops still loyal to Caesar in fighting against Brutus and his new Masters. After a year, Brutus was defeated, and the Vampyres slaughtered him in a rage. The history books say he took his own life. That just isn't true.

For a time, Caesar's three most loyal allies formed the second triumvirate, but as soon as they were truly turning the tide against the Vampyres, they began to disagree on how to proceed. This led to further disagreements on how to govern, and finally, the rift between them became irreparable. Marc Antony left with his new wife, Cleopatra, and their child (officially called Caesar's child for political reasons), and Marcus Lepidus fought with Octavian.

Octavian was the clear winner and decided that even though he loved Marc Antony, he could not afford to divide the Empire when they were so close to defeating the Vampyres. Knowing that they would have to fight their friend Octavian, Marc Antony and Cleopatra took their own lives.

Octavian took the official name Octavian Julius Caesar, and it became a tradition for every Roman Emperor to take the name of Caesar after that. Even the Germanic Kaiser and the Russian Czars based their title on Caesar. This was because they had joined the fight against the Vampyres and took Gaius Julius Caesar's cause for themselves. Every Roman Emperor from then until the end of the Empire was sworn to fight the Vampyre threat. This explains many things, from Nero's burning of Rome to the fall of the Empire brought on by the machinations of the Vampyres.

Much of the world's history can thus be attributed to them, but that is another story.

Author's Note

I came up with the origin story of the Vampyres around 2001 and had it milling about in my mind for years. I devised the idea for the Julius Caesar story around 2008 while reading *Rubicon: The Last Years of The Roman Republic* by Tom Holland. I decided to make myself smarter on the subject and read more books, including (but not limited to):

The Assassination of Julius Caesar, A People's History of Rome by Michael Parenti

Caesar, Life of a Colossus by Adrian Goldsworthy

The Way of Caesar by Irwin Isenberg

The Civil War by Julius Caesar (translated by F.P. Long)

Caesar, a Biography by Christian Meier

A Day in the Life of Ancient Rome by Alberto Angela (translated by Gregory Conti)

Roman Warfare by Adrian Goldsworthy

Ancient Rome: A Military and Political History by Christopher S. Mackey

The Mammoth Book of Eyewitness: Ancient Rome Collection and Editorial Materials by J. Lewis-Stempel, Edited by Jon E. Lewis

I have tried hard not to steal anyone's words, but I often referred to all these books while writing. Where books disagreed on the history or timetable, I picked and chose what fit my narrative. Although I did try to be as historically accurate as possible, this is primarily a work of fiction, not a historical text. If I got some things wrong, it may have been my misunderstanding, or it may have been by design to make my narrative work.

I recently watched a show about Caesar's life in a dramatized documentary style and was amazed at how much was left out completely or glossed over. This made me feel better about my manipulation of history.

I would love to read reviews and feedback about this book. It is my first, and very short. It was also started in 2008 and left alone for years at a time with sporadic attempts to complete it. At last, I decided to sit down and finish it. I got out the story I wanted to tell in far fewer words than expected.

I intend to write the origin story of my Vampyres next and perhaps tell some more tales of how Vampyres have influenced history. Unfortunately, someone beat me to Abraham Lincoln's story, but there are many more to tell.

As a separate note, several people reading this for me as I wrote commented on the Julian calendar, mainly in disbelief that Julius Caesar "invented" our calendar. He did, in fact, implement the calendar almost as we know it today. The Julian calendar was 365.25 days. This made the 365-day year with a one-additional-day leap year work out evenly. We now use the Gregorian calendar, which is 365.2425 days long. We do NOT have a leap year EVERY fourth year. Years divisible by 100 are not leap years ... unless they are divisible by 400, then they are again. (In other words, there is a difference of three days every 400 years.) This is a more confusing but also more accurate way to keep us in line with a solar year. The Gregorian calendar was implemented in 1582 by Pope Gregory XIII as a way to stop the date of Easter from drifting too far from the vernal equinox. As I write this, the date is 28 December 2023 by the Gregorian calendar, but 12 December 2023 by the Julian calendar. You're welcome.

Acknowledgments

Special thanks to my Kickstarter backers:

Josh G.

Brent Longfellow

Jordan Schreck

Stacey Atkins

Belauna Dietz

Warren

Ryan

Jace the Ace

Hank Hayden

I also want to acknowledge Linda, Andy, and the folks at Cup and Quill for such great feedback and timely editing. Without you this project would be something less.

Finally, I need to acknowledge Wikipedia, PBS, World History Encyclopedia, vroma.org, biography.com, the History Channel, and countless books, websites, and teachers.

Wendy and Richard Pini, Neil Gaiman, Jody Houser, China Mieville, and countless other authors.

D&D, Kids on Bikes, Whitewolf, Pathfinder, Call of Cthulhu, and countless other TTRPGs.

All these things fostered my knowledge and imagination and inspired me to want to write.